MIDNIGHT HOUR

Celia Rees lives in Leamington Spa with her husband and daughter. She taught English in comprehensive schools for sixteen years, and now divides her time between lecturing and writing. Her novels have the excitement and story-telling power of adult thrillers, but with teenagers as the central characters.

Midnight Hour is Celia Rees's fifth novel. *The Bailey Game* and *Colour Her Dead* are also published by Macmillan.

Also by Celia Rees

The Bailey Game
Colour Her Dead

MIDNIGHT HOUR

Celia Rees

MACMILLAN
CHILDREN'S BOOKS

First published 1997 by Macmillan Children's Books
a division of Macmillan Publishers Limited
25 Eccleston Place, London SW1W 9NF
and Basingstoke

Associated companies throughout the world

ISBN 0 330 34429 3

1 3 5 7 9 8 6 4 2

A CIP catalogue record for this book is available from
the British Library.

Printed and bound in Great Britain by
Mackays of Chatham plc, Kent

For my daughter, Catrin

Chapter 1

There was not much in Amanda McCann's mind as she rode home from the university that mid-March evening. The thoughts in her head could have been shared by any student in the land: meeting her friends, fitting work into a busy weekend, making her money stretch. The end of term was looming and there were bills to pay, deadlines to meet. One particular worry, an assignment, to be handed in Monday morning, began to take priority as she pedalled on. Her thinking might have followed quite different lines if she had known she would never see another Monday. She would never hand the project in, never write it. The moment she cycled out of the campus, the rest of her life could be counted in hours.

Mercia University was very large. A campus the size of a small town occupied a sprawling site on the western edge of the biggest city in the Midlands. Amanda was a PE student in the Institute of Education. A bit of a fitness fanatic, she rarely missed the Friday night aerobics class, but this made her later than usual. At the unmanned barrier, which marked the end of the University's own road system, she stopped to switch her lights on against the growing dark.

She checked the battery-operated red flash on the back of her jacket and adjusted the strap of her helmet. Amanda was careful about things like that: her own health and safety, her visibility to other road users. It is strange how people are cautious in some things, but not in others. Amanda's chosen route home avoided the obvious hazards of heavy traffic and choking pollution on the great arterial roads which led past the university, but the way she took was lonely. Distant high rise flats, serrating the horizon, were the nearest human habitation. Her journey took her along Wheeler's Lane, a little-frequented byroad, past a disused aerodrome and on through one of the remaining pockets of countryside to survive around the outskirts of the vast West Midlands conurbation.

She rounded a corner, on the last stretch now, scarcely a mile from the home she shared with two other third-year students. The house brought another thought to mind. One she had been trying to avoid. She'd received something else today. It had come in the morning post. A compact disc. A compilation of blues tracks, some of them dating way back. The gift was as mysterious and inexplicable as the one before it, and the one before that. She didn't like that kind of music, didn't even have a CD player. She changed gear, ready for the hill.

Her friends thought it was funny. They teased her about a secret admirer. At first she had joined in with the laughter, had even been flattered, but she had soon ceased to find it amusing. Valentine's day had come and gone and still the cards kept arriving. She was beginning to dread the postman's footsteps on the path, his ring on the bell.

There had been requests for her, dedications, in clubs, on the student radio, even one of those tacky 'Our Tune' features. Amanda found herself checking every male, everywhere she went, to see if he might be watching her. Even men in the street couldn't pass by without her thinking: is this the guy? Is he the one? It was beginning to really get to her, to be honest, but she could hardly go to the police and complain because someone kept sending her flowers.

Her friends thought it was a fellow student. If you included the Institute where she was, the university proper, and the teaching hospital, that narrowed it down to about ten thousand people. When the presents first began to arrive, she had assumed the sender was known to her, one of her so-called friends playing a joke on her. Now she realized it could be anyone. A stranger. That was scary. She pedalled faster as the bike took the straight.

Up ahead of her, across the tarmac, lay a thin nylon cord. Its pale colour had been deliberately dirtied to make it almost invisible; she would never see it in the fading light. The cord was attached to a tree on the opposite side of the road, tied at a level to hit about chest height. She was travelling at speed, so it must not catch her round the neck. He did not want her damaged. Yet.

His eyes flicked to where his van was parked just inside a field. He'd picked the spot with care. It was just yards away, but the tall tangled hedge cut off any view from the road and the muddy entrance to the field was a mess of different tracks. Popular spot at night, lovers used it all the time. The thinner tyres of cars crossed and re-crossed the thick ruts made by tractors. He checked his jacket. It was the kind that wouldn't look out of place in the countryside; the hood hid his face and there were plenty of pockets. His hands fluttered over them now, feeling the hard bulge of the Stanley knife, the stiff circle of rope. Inside the poacher's pocket lay a ski mask, with sewn up mouth and eyes, and wide black electrical tape. This had been cut into neatly measured lengths to provide a gag, in case she tried to cry out, and manacles for wrists and ankles. Success depended on planning, on knowing exactly what was going to happen. He loved to see the surge of surprise, the pupils expand wide, when the hood was finally peeled back from their eyes.

She was near now. He could hear the wheels of her bike. He breathed deeply, poised like a diver on the very edge of the moment, striving for absolute control. The circle of light cast by her lamp illuminated the road. He counted the seconds in his head. She was almost parallel.

Suddenly he was covered in sweat. Fluorescent stripes flashed green and white on her jacket. After so much waiting the adrenalin coursed through his system, making his actions sudden and precise. He pulled the line tight, bringing the rider down. Her helmet hit the road surface with a flat crack and she lay, dazed and winded, tangled in the twisted wheels of her bicycle. He looked down at her, feeling the power rising within him. Excitement vibrated along nerves as taut as piano wire, resonating through him, singing like the blood inside his head, as he stepped out from his hiding place.

Right first time, Amanda. You know me all right. Well enough to say 'hello', to pass the time of day, share the odd joke, before you go off with your friends. You are about to know me a whole lot better. He released the catch on her cycle helmet and wrenched it off. Her dark hair tumbled free, luxuriant and thick. He felt the silkiness between his fingers. That was what had attracted him in the first instance. He touched her head; it moved limp on her neck but she was still breathing. Her hair fell back. He caressed the creamy soft skin, tracing the lines of her face with a fingernail, following the high cheekbone, down the jaw from ear to chin. She was lovely. A lovely looking girl. That was what had kept him interested. *You think you are something special, don't you, baby? Well, I got news for you.* She began to moan, she was coming round. He began to hum, high and nasal, an old blues tune . . . ***you ain't called, momma, lef' me all alone*** . . . He chanted to himself as he twisted tape round her head . . . ***you been a bad girl, baby, gonna bring you home*** . . . He quickly secured her hands and feet . . . ***ain't joking, momma, just you wait and see, gonna do everything that you done to me*** . . .

He slapped her, hard, until her eyes fully opened. Irises pale blue, ringed by indigo, a very unusual colour; her eyes were her best feature. They stared wide and confused, then recognition flared, of him, the gag, everything, all in one dilation. He smiled down at her, continuing his high humming, swaying to the song playing inside his head. *You never guessed, did you? Never guessed the thoughts that lay behind this friendly face, these smiling eyes. Never guessed how much they knew about your life* . . . ***right around midnight, you're gonna get the news*** . . . *Don't struggle* . . . ***you been a bad girl, momma, time to pay your dues*** . . . He punched her. Quick jabs. Once. Twice. *I said, don't struggle!*

She fell back, unconscious. He hauled her to her feet and threw her into the back of the van, along with her helmet and cycle, everything from the scene. He would get rid of the bike later on, dump it in a different district. No one would know where she'd gone. No one would know where she'd been. He knelt over her, not singing now, speaking the words near, a harsh whispering into her ear . . . ***You hurt me so bad, baby*** . . . He wrenched her arms back and pulled her feet up ... ***hurt me so bad, baby*** ... He tied them together so the harder she fought the tighter the rope would bind her ... ***so bad, baby, give me the killing time blues*** ...

Chapter 2

'Large fries, Whopper, chocolate shake.' The girl recited, already eyeing the queue behind him.

'That's right,' he replied, smiling.

The girl paused. 'Eat in, or take out?'

'Eat in.' His eyes crinkled. He had a nice smile. She found herself smiling back.

He took his meal to the window and bit into his burger. Amanda McCann. He did not have to think about her any more. Another girl had disappeared. So many do every year. She was nobody. No body. They would search for a while but they would never find her. Without a body she would become just another statistic, like the others had done before her. He sucked on his shake. He felt good. He always did afterwards. Mellow and relaxed.

He stared out at the newly developed green-field site. These seemed to be springing up all round the edges of the city: Leisure Centre, Megabowl, Toys 'R' Us and Do It All. Right in front of him a multiplex cinema gleamed white in the spring sunshine. Chance had brought him here. He had been driving around, cruising the city, when he found himself approaching the tangled skeins of a motorway junction. A glance out of the van window had shown him a Burger King and triggered sudden, overwhelming hunger. Relish oozed, thick and red, down the sides of his mouth and on to his chin. He did not eat junk food as a rule, and red meat hardly at all. Today was an exception. He demolished the whole meal in a couple of wolfish bites. No one noticed his speed and greed, they were used to it here.

He wiped his fingers on the waxed paper and his mouth on a paper napkin. Moustache. He would shave that off. Personal preference. He had no fear of it being an identifying feature.

He disposed of the trash and headed for the door. Billboards studded the white walls of the multiplex opposite. He looked up, and his legs seemed to give. Blair Paige. He studied the face of the young British actress. Still in her teens, she was the girl of the moment, the focus of so many dreams.

DEGREES OF DIFFICULTY

Underneath, the banner read:

Coming Soon

This film was bringing her to him. Its release had been delayed, controversy engulfing the movie like a tidal wave, but when the film premiered, she would be here. That time was near.

Normally he didn't believe in omens and portents, but the factors aligning were too strong to be dismissed. Fate was intervening. He had been waiting for this.

He stared up at the poster. This film was right for her. Its subject absolutely appropriate. He had not liked her last one, *Born to Kill*, too brash, too violent, too tacky. Besides, she had bleached her hair for the part, cut it short. She was different now: dark hair tumbling, blue eyes huge, in a perfect face. She had the looks he most coveted.

His thoughts ran on through his fractured mind. The face seemed to change, the smile turning into a sneer, the look she was giving was sparking up his anger. She was staring past him, looking straight though him, full lips pouted, showing contempt, as if she was too good for him, like he was too small and insignificant, beneath her notice. He would have to teach her. He would have to let her know.

There were other reasons. His mind switched track. The other girls. Heather, Kay and Amanda. They had been just as pretty, just hadn't had her chances. Down in the cold earth there would be no stars. He would be doing it for them as well.

And he'd be doing it for her. Even a body as superb as that would sag, gain fat, her flawless face become lined and bagged. Eventually even Blair Paige would age and change. This way she would be like James Dean, Marilyn Monroe. She would never grow old. She would always be this young, this beautiful. He felt the familiar adrenalin rush and his breath became shallow.

Cars started up round him. People were coming out of the cinema, but he stood absolutely still. He felt like a god. He would make Blair Paige famous for ever.

Chapter 3

'Blair, Blair! Leonora's here.'

Gina Paige shouted to her daughter for the second time. Getting no reply, she returned to the hall mirror, checking her make-up, frowning at the little crow's-foot lines round her eyes. Must have something done about them, time for another visit to Dr Bronsky. She delicately applied a wetted little finger to the corner of her lipsticked mouth. Behind her, reflected in the mirror, Leonora Quinn stood in the middle of the parquet floor, clutching her briefcase.

'What a lovely house,' Leonora commented, looking round the cavernous reception hall with its gold-framed pictures and walnut panelling.

'Yes, isn't it?' Gina turned to Blair's guest. 'We have it rented, just for a month. Blair needed rest, to get out of the limelight.'

Leonora nodded. She read the papers like everybody else.

'Blair wanted to come here,' Gina added to explain the location. To most people in show-business, anywhere outside London seemed eccentric. 'It's as good a place as any, I guess.'

The other woman nodded again. 'Don't you come from round here? Originally, I mean? Sedgebrook. That's near here.'

'Yes.' Gina frowned. 'How do you know that?'

'I have her birthchart.' Leonora indicated the

briefcase. She was one of the country's leading astrologers, her forecasts syndicated in daily newspapers.

'Of course.' Gina's smile thinned.

She was careful not to draw attention to Blair's humble origins. To have been born in boring suburbia, on the outskirts of the British Midlands' biggest city – there were more glamorous starts in life.

'Let me help you.' She went over to help Leonora out of her mackintosh. 'July!' Gina gestured in mock despair as she shook off the drops. 'I'd almost forgotten about the weather! Now, if we were back in LA, cloudless sky, sun all the time . . .' She gave an exaggerated shrug. 'Here, let me . . .'

She went to take Leonora's briefcase, but the other woman snatched it back. What did she carry in there that was so precious? Her ridiculous charts? A pack of Tarot cards? Why couldn't Blair have her forecast, or whatever it was, faxed to her? Why invite the woman to the house? She cursed the idiot in Hollywood who had encouraged this astrology business.

'I'll just go and see where Blair is,' Gina said, her smile straining further.

Where was the girl? Gina went towards the stairs. If Blair invited this woman, she should be here to meet her. Gina did not intend to spend any more time chatting about the weather with her daughter's pet astrologer.

'Blair!' she shouted up the stairs again.

Still no reply. All she could hear was music dinning away somewhere. Movie star or no, sometimes Blair acted like any other teenager.

'Blair?'

Gina stepped over Blair's muddy trainers and picked a way through peeled-off jogging kit.

Music played loud from the next room and the shower hissed. Gina put her head round the door and shouted:

'Blair! That woman's here.'

'So? I can't exactly see her like this, can I?'

Blair stepped out of the shower and Gina was struck again, as she had been so many times, by her beauty, her perfection.

'What are you staring at? Give me a chance to get dressed. I'll be with you in a minute.'

Gina withdrew and wandered round the bedroom. Most mothers know the kind of pride that says their child is exceptional, something special, but for most people that sense of specialness fades as their child lapses into the ordinary. Not for Gina. From the day that Blair was born, Isabel Jane Franklin, in Sedgebrook General Hospital, Gina knew her daughter was going to be quite remarkable.

Blair had an agent before she was out of nappies. She was on the books of the best model agencies by the time she was three, and the work had just poured in. TV adverts, magazines, catalogues – any showcase to display her astonishing beauty. Back then it had been mainly modelling. The acting came later.

First, adverts and children's TV, then bit parts in adult movies. Blair showed considerable flair; she had talent, they said, a natural in front of the camera. That was where the future lay, Gina decided. With that came the change of name. Franklin belonged to her husband. That went. Isabel Jane had been his choice. That went too. Replaced by Blair. Gina chose it, a shortening of Bel Air – because that was where they were heading. Paige was her own name before she married.

Blair got larger and larger parts, the new name working like magic. Then came the big break. *The Photographer.* Blair was twelve at the time, the same age as the child in the film, and was Oscar-nominated for her playing of the autistic daughter of the photographer's housekeeper. There had been a certain amount of nudity but, within the context of the film, it was perfectly justifiable. There had been accusations, from certain sections of the press, of child abuse, even pornography. All nonsense, of course – Blair had been protected at every step – but the extra publicity had turned a small serious art-house movie into a hit.

Since then, Blair had not looked back. She had worked steadily, her career seldom faltering under Gina's astute guidance and careful management. Gina had first and last say, and chose each project carefully. Some of Blair's films were controversial, but so what? The more controversy a film attracted, the more it took at the box office.

Her latest, *Degrees of Difficulty,* dealt with another dangerous subject: a young diver's intense relationship with her coach in the lead-up to the Olympics. The combination of a very young girl – Blair played younger than her actual age – and a much older man, led some of the tabloids to dub the film 'Olympic Lolita'. The movie had only just won release in Britain, for that reason, and had been denied a licence in some countries, but those things did not matter to Gina. Blair played opposite an actor/director whose name alone was enough to sell the film. Once again, Gina's choice was impeccable. The film had just won the *Palme d'Or* at Cannes and was going to give her daughter the star status Gina craved.

They had just finished an exhausting round of interviews and publicity. Retreat to this rented mansion had been partly Blair's idea, but not entirely. Gina knew the danger of over-exposure. Keep 'em hungry. Melting into anonymity only added to the mystique and, let's face it, you could not get more anonymous than this particular stretch of Britain's heartland. This place was as good as any to plan the next move, to take stock. But you could be in London within the hour, that was the beauty of it.

She stopped in front of a picture of Stephen, Blair's brother. He was the other reason for them being here; it was a chance to see Stephen, a chance for them all to be together.

When Gina left with Blair for the US, Stephen

had stayed with his father. He had retained his father's name. A handsome boy, he and Blair had the same blue eyes and dark hair. As children the two of them had shared modelling assignments. They had looked so cute together, a winning combination. She looked down at her son's adult face. That was before his father had kicked in with his own plans for him. Stephen was studying medicine now at the teaching hospital attached to Mercia University.

They still looked alike, even though Blair was seventeen and Stephen was twenty-two. He was a man now, not a boy, Gina had to remind herself. She seemed to have missed him growing up. Where had it gone, that time in between? All those years, while they had lived in America because of Blair's career, he had spent here. Had he missed out? Of course not. If he had done, it was his father's fault. She dismissed any trace of anxiety from her own mind. He'd had one of the best educations it was possible to buy, thanks to Blair's money.

Blair came back into the room, towelling her hair.

'What are you thinking about?' she said, as she moved in front of the mirror.

'I was just thinking about Stephen.'

'What about him?'

'I was hoping he'd come and stay, not just drop in now and again. We've hardly seen him.'

'He has his own life, Gina.' Blair began sorting through her make-up. 'You can't expect him to drop everything just because we are here. He'll come when he wants to.'

When they arrived in England, Stephen had been there to meet them at Heathrow and had stayed at their London hotel, but just for a few days. He had cut the visit short suddenly, leaving a note at reception saying he had to get back. He'd been once or twice to see them at this house, but had only stayed an hour or so each time. Gina found his behaviour puzzling, but Blair had more of an insight. Stephen was quiet, unassuming. He was not used to all the fuss and razzmatazz that surrounded her public life and, apart from that, he had a hard time dealing with Gina.

'I blame that girlfriend,' her mother was saying. 'She's changed him. He never used to be like that – so off-hand. I don't think she's good for him. Too possessive and jealous. Girls like that are nothing but trouble.'

'How do you know that, Gina?' Blair applied a lick or two of mascara. 'You've never even met her.'

'I can tell by her tone when she answers the phone. She can hardly utter a civil word.'

'You can tell Leonora she can come up now.'

'Leonora?'

'Quinn. Downstairs?'

'Oh, yes. Why are you seeing her, anyway?'

'My business.'

Blair turned back to the mirror and Gina left, dismissed. She went back down the stairs, biting back her annoyance. Blair was the only person in the world who could treat her that way. Why did she put up with it? Blair had no right to keep things private. She wouldn't be where she was today if it wasn't for her mother. Even the gossip columnists were careful to acknowledge that. They ignored Gina Paige at their peril.

It's not *my* job to carry messages back and forth, she thought, her mood thoroughly soured now. Where was Felicity, for goodness' sake? What was a PA for?

'Sorry to keep you waiting.' She addressed Leonora from the bottom of the stairs. 'Blair will see you now. First on the right.' *Make your own way there,* she added under her breath, *you're the psychic.*

Gina went to the sitting room window and stared out at the immaculate lawn sweeping down to the river. The day was getting worse, if anything, wind and rain battering the panes, but that did not matter. Gina had her own reasons for renting this big old house. 'Millionaire's Row' is what local people used to call this road. It was in Ashbury, an exclusive village, a few miles further into the country from Sedgebrook, where Gina had once lived. She used to wheel Blair out in her pushchair and head up here, walking along past the beautiful houses set back in their own grounds, dreaming, scheming, eaten up by envy. Well, here I am. She smiled. Portland House was the best of the lot. Time to award herself a gin and tonic.

Swimming pool, sauna – you name it, this house had got it. Blair had wanted a gym, but had settled for the next best thing: The Greswoldes Health Club was the neighbouring property. Blair was obsessive about her fitness: jogging every morning with her personal trainer, working out every afternoon. It had started with the film, *Degrees of Difficulty.* Blair had wanted to perform the diving sequences herself, only allowing a double for the most difficult actions. Gina had thought this totally unnecessary – what were doubles for? But Blair had insisted, much to the delight of the director, an action film veteran who still performed all his own stunts.

In a strange way, Blair had been right. Her virtuoso performance on the diving boards, the beautiful balletic way it had been shot, added to the film's attraction. It also took some of the attention away from the other scenes, the ones in bed, the ones where they did have to use a body double.

'These have arrived.' Felicity, Blair's personal assistant, cut into Gina's thoughts. 'I just found them outside.'

The tall young woman in her late twenties stood at the door holding a bouquet of roses, mixed red and white.

Felicity always looked immaculate, elegantly dressed, her blonde hair smoothed back in a chignon. She and Gina did not always get on, but Felicity's cool common sense and reserved English manner made a refreshing change from some of the studio's brash young Americans. She had worked with Blair for a number of years and was almost like a big sister, fiercely loyal and very protective.

'I didn't hear a van . . .' Gina turned, questioning.

'Neither did I . . .'

Felicity frowned. Through the blooms, her wide-apart grey eyes were giving out danger signals. The bouquet had clearly been professionally arranged. Judging by the quality of the flowers and the length of the stems they must have been expensive, and yet she had not heard a florist's van. The bouquet had just appeared on the doorstep, as if by magic.

'Who are they for? Me or Blair?' Gina asked.

'There's no card.' Felicity parted the clouds of gypsophila.

'They can't have just appeared. Get on to security.'

'I already have,' Felicity replied. 'Just now. When I first found them. They don't know anything about it.'

'Let me speak to them.'

Gina was already reaching for the phone. She punched in an internal number and waited for someone to answer. Her mood, fuelled by fear, escalated to fury. Security was top priority. She had insisted on it when they took this place. The Studio had insisted on it. A young star like Blair, rising to prominence, right in the public eye, could so easily become the focus of unwanted attention. Stalker attention. There had been a spate of cases, both sides of the Atlantic. Gina pressed security's number again. Given the kind of film Blair was in, you couldn't be too careful.

This address was supposed to be secret; nevertheless, they had taken no chances. The house was not only fully alarmed, it had electronic gates, manned at all times, and video surveillance equipment installed. The firm employed was supposed to be the best in the area. What was going on here?

'Hello? Belmont Security. Barry speaking.' A male voice answered, the distinctive local accent whining through the crackle of the mobile. 'How can I help you?'

Gina explained, words dropping like acid into the phone. 'We've just had flowers delivered to the front door of the house. There is no card with them, and we heard no van. So I'd like to know how they got here . . . You have no idea!' Gina barked back. 'What about the gates? The video? . . . Teething problems!' she screeched. 'What teething problems? We've been here a week! And you had a week before that!'

'Rain. Temporarily shorted some of the systems.' The voice droned. 'We're on to it now . . .'

'Now's not good enough!'

'No one unauthorized has entered these grounds, Mrs Paige. I can assure you of that.'

'How did these flowers get here, then? Parachute? You lot better sharpen up – or I'll be getting somebody else. I can assure *you* of that!'

Barry White returned the phone to his inside pocket, Gina's tirade buzzing in his ear. He was standing by the entrance to the drive, rain sluicing down his uniform. The gates were stuck at half open, the video cameras blind and immobile. In his pocket his hand squeezed rhythmically, nervously grasping a pair of pliers. The wires had been cut. Severed clean through at the side of the house. But he wasn't about to tell her that. She'd have him sacked in a minute. It might only pay a few lousy quid an hour, but it was a job and he intended to keep it. He tipped the water off his cap and trudged back down the drive to repair the damage.

Crisis over, Gina returned to the bar to freshen her drink. She was just awarding herself an extra tot when there was a strangled cry from the hall. Blair's voice followed:

'Leonora! What's wrong? Felicity! Get a glass of water!'

Gina went out into the hall to find her daughter kneeling in front of the astrologer.

'It's the flowers,' Felicity explained, handing the glass to Blair. 'Leonora's had some kind of reaction.'

Leonora Quinn took the crystal glass in both hands, but the water was spilling before it reached her lips. Blair had to help her drink.

'Get them out of the house!' she managed to splutter. 'Now. Immediately!'

'Why, Leonora?'

The astrologer could not reply. Sudden nausea was gripping her like a vice.

'Not you!' She uttered through gritted teeth as Blair went to do her bidding. 'One of the others. You must not touch them!'

'Better do as she says.'

Blair indicated for Felicity to take the flowers away.

Immediately they were removed, Leonora seemed to recover.

'I felt a presence. Something malevolent,' she said, as Blair showed her out. 'The hand of one who means you harm.'

'What was that all about?' Gina asked when Blair came back.

'You tell me,' Blair shrugged. 'Who were those flowers from, anyway?'

'They've only just arrived.' Gina replied vaguely.

She did not really want to discuss this. There was no need to alert Blair. Yet.

'Where are you going?' she asked instead.

Blair was dressed to go out.

'I thought I'd go and see Louise.'

'Louise Morgan?' Gina asked, incredulous.

Louise and Blair had grown up together. They had been neighbours, living practically next door to each other. They had been like sisters, insepar-able. Until the ages of nine and ten, when Gina's ambitions had taken her own daughter far from ordinary little girls like Louise.

'Where does she live now?'

'In Sedgebrook, where she always did,' Blair replied, 'where we used to live. Remember?'

Of course she did. It was only seven years ago, but when Gina looked back, her memories seemed to belong to another lifetime.

'What on earth do you want to go and see her for?'

'Because she's my friend,' Blair replied, zipping up her coat. 'And I promised I would.' She picked up the keys to Felicity's car. 'And also I want to. Enough reasons?'

'I suppose so.'

Gina was dubious about this. Blair did not need old associations, they only became a nuisance. Sometimes, however, it was best not to interfere, to let Blair have her head, and Gina sensed this was one of those occasions. She could always deal with the girl and destroy the friendship later.

'You can put those keys back.' Gina pointed to the table. 'You can't drive yourself. You will have to be driven.'

'Of course I can. My licence is valid . . .' Blair started to protest. Then she stopped. 'Something's happened,' she said in a different voice. 'Hasn't it?'

Her mother waved the question aside and turned away to summon the chauffeur. Blair put the keys slowly back on the hall table, and waited for the car to arrive, frustration building inside her. Something had happened and it had to do with those flowers. Plenty of things told her, not just Leonora and her reaction – she could tell by Gina's mood, by the looks passing between her and Felicity. But neither of them would admit anything, even under direct questioning. Blair was tired of being treated like that, kept in the dark all the time, every little bit of her life regulated, for her own good, for her own safety. Felicity could be all right, but in matters like this she and Gina closed ranks. Blair needed someone else here. Someone on her side, someone she could trust. She'd planned on it being Stephen, but he never stayed long enough. Blair smiled, suddenly wanting to see Louise for a whole lot of reasons.

Chapter 4

A couple of miles away, Louise Morgan lay in bed. She was alone in the house; her family had all left for work or school.

Silence except for rain slapping the window. It was unseasonably cold for mid-July and outside looked grey and uninviting. Not that it mattered. Louise had no plans. She yawned and closed her eyes. It was nice to have nowhere to go, nothing to do except doze and listen to the radio. Luxury.

Eventually conscience got the better of her. Downstairs, in the hall, she glanced at the list of chores left by her mother, and then up to the mirror, holding her hair up at the back, turning her head this way and that. She should be thinking about looking for work – Dad had scrawled 'GET A JOB!' under 'put washing on' and 'do breakfast dishes' – instead she was wondering whether to get her hair cut, or maybe coloured, add red, or something exciting, to her natural dark blonde. It was such a nothing colour. She frowned, unable to make up her mind. It was the sort of thing that needed a second opinion and there wasn't anyone around to ask.

Suddenly she missed school. Having your hair cut was the kind of thing to discuss on the bus, but that wouldn't be until next autumn. GCSEs were over, the last exam had fallen on her sixteenth birthday. Louise felt a knotting in the pit of her stomach; all she could do now was wait for the results. Maybe she could give someone a call, go into town, but there was no one around at the moment. Most of her friends had gone on vacation or had got themselves holiday jobs.

She leaned in close to her reflection. Her eyes were a bit of a nothing colour, too, not really grey, or green or blue. Perhaps she should get colour contact lenses. Not because she needed them, but for cosmetic reasons. What with? Money was tight at the moment. There were no holidays planned for this summer and the job hunt had not got very far. Or anywhere. There weren't enough jobs and it was probably too late. She should have got organized ages ago.

Louise let her hair fall back as another thought presented itself. Maybe Della could help. Even if she didn't have anything, she might know someone who did. There were other businesses in her building. The school hadn't been exactly ecstatic about Louise doing her work experience at a detective agency, but she had loved every minute. Her own enthusiasm had been reflected in Della's glowing report. When it was time to leave, she had said:

'Any time I can help. Just give me a call.'

It was worth a try. Why hadn't she thought of it before? Louise padded off to retrieve the business card from where she kept it tucked inside her personal organizer.

'Hi. FemTec Investigation Agency. There's no

one here right now, but if you'd like to leave your message, name, and number . . .'

'Er, hi. This is Louise Morgan. Remember? I'm, er, I'm . . .' Louise closed her eyes. She hated talking to answer machines, but stopping in mid-sentence would be really stupid. She made herself go on. 'I'm looking for a holiday job, and I was, was just wondering if you, you know, knew of anything. If so, could you let me know? My number is 0121705 . . .'

Louise gabbled out the rest of the number and put the phone down quickly.

The letter box flapped. Louise went to see if there was anything interesting. There might be a card from Blair. She was in the country – Louise had seen her on the television, in the newspapers – but so far she had not been in touch. Louise felt depression descending. Blair had promised, but maybe this time she would not bother. There had been no reply to the last letter. Louise had written regularly over the years, long letters full of feelings, frustrations, hopes and fears, as well as mundane details about school. Blair never wrote back at any great length, but she always sent something.

It felt strange to have such a famous friend. Louise could remember when they were just the same, two little girls playing in the road. Then Gina had taken Blair away and all Louise could do was watch from home as the other girl's career grew bigger and bigger and the reactions changed from 'Blair who?' to 'No kidding! Really?'

Not that she talked about it all that much. This friendship with Blair was something she preferred to keep to herself. It was not just the occasional spiteful responses; Blair had gone so far, it was as though she actually was in another galaxy. Louise could no longer imagine what her life was really like, behind what she read in magazines or gossip columns. Their friendship was bound to fade. It had to end. The distance between them would become just too great for any relationship to be sustained. After all, as her own friends pointed out, what on earth could Blair Paige see in her?

One of the people to say that was Matt. Boyfriend. Ex-boyfriend. There might be a card from him. Or even a letter. Wanting them to get back together. If there was, she would tear it up. Read it, and then tear it up? Keep it to cry over? Much more likely. Not any more. Positive thinking had made her phone Della. If it worked for one thing, it might work for another.

The doorbell, ringing above, made her jump. A dark shape leaned forward, filling the frosted glass. The bell rang again and the shape stepped back. Louise stood up and reached for the latch. Must be the postman with a parcel, or something he'd forgotten.

'Hello?'

It wasn't the postman; she could tell that, but not much else. The person was standing facing away from her. Stevedore's hat pulled right down, biker's boots and an oversize jacket.

'Hello yourself.' The reply came back.

'Blair? My God! It is you, isn't it?'

Blair Paige swept off her cap. Thick dark hair fell in waves, framing her face, making her look like her pictures.

'Of course it is. Well? Aren't you going to ask me in?'

The smile widened, blazing up to her eyes. Blair stepped into the house and hugged Louise, picking her up off her feet.

'Not expecting visitors, then?'

She held her friend at arm's length. Louise looked down at her wrinkled pyjamas.

'Now you come to mention it, no I wasn't. Not you of all people. I'm so glad to see you . . .'

Louise lapsed into silence, staring at Blair, not quite able to believe she was really there, that this was really happening.

'Me too.' Blair held her close for a moment and kissed her cheek.

'Really, honestly?'

'Really. Honestly.'

Blair flashed the famous smile again, but it was tempered by a tenderness that was rarely seen, on or off the screen.

Louise laughed and Blair asked, 'What's funny?'

'Nothing. Just glad, that's all.'

Blair laughed then and, as they went into the kitchen, the distance between them dwindled into nothing.

'So what's it *really* like – life in Hollywood?' Louise asked.

'Oh, there's all the premieres and receptions, things you have to go to, then there's clubs and – it's one mad party after another.' The beautiful mouth took on an ironic twist and Blair shook her head as she sipped her coffee. 'It's not like that. I don't go out all that much.' She gave an elegant shrug. 'It's just, you know, just ordinary.'

No, Louise didn't know. She failed to think of a suitable reply. All that wealth. Blair did the kind of things, led the kind of life, that most people just see on TV, or read about in magazines. Louise felt a chasm breaking in the ground between them. To her it was almost too much to imagine, to Blair it was just 'ordinary'.

'Most of them,' Blair was saying, 'are totally self-obsessed and superficial – and they'd see that as a compliment.'

'What about Drew Chambers?' Louise mentioned her co-star in *Born to Kill*. 'He's *really* fit!'

Blair laughed. 'He's as stupid as the kid he played on screen.' She leaned back in her chair. 'Don't believe everything you read. Most of these liaisons are engineered, set up by the studio publicity machine, or Gina. She's got a calendar. Honest to God! It's like, "Oh, Blair ought to go out on a date, must fix that up." Then she makes a call and ticks it off. I'm not joking!'

Louise leaned on the table, chin resting on her hands.

'All those letters from me,' she said quietly.

'Full of school and trivia and stuff. Must seem really boring.'

'Not at all.' Blair leaned towards her. 'Sometimes you seem like the only person with a real life. I don't know what I'd do if you stopped writing. All the things you say kind of keep me in touch with reality.'

'Do you want some toast? I was just about to make some.'

'Yeah, OK.'

Louise buttered toast and sat down at the table.

'Hey, this is good!' Blair said with her mouth full. 'Must be the butter. I almost never eat it . . .'

Blair chattered on about diet as she finished one piece and started on another. Louise put her own slice down as a thought began to nag, taking away her appetite. Blair might be behaving like any friend, but she wasn't just any friend. She was a star, with a million things to do, a million important people to see. *So what exactly is she doing here, sitting eating toast, at this particular kitchen table, with me?*

There was something else. Louise began to see past her own anxiety, to notice Blair's tension. She had finished eating now and her thin fingers were shredding crusts, drawing patterns in the resulting crumbs. When she pushed the plate away, they began to drum out inaudible chords on the edge of the table.

'We make each other nervous,' Blair said after a while. 'That's a good sign. Chatting away, drinking coffee, eating toast and all the time you're wondering if I've got too big for you to be a friend of mine and I'm wondering if you'll still like me.' She smiled. 'At least we care enough to worry.'

'Well, have you? Got too big, I mean?'

'I'm here, aren't I?'

'I was just about to ask you why.'

'You're important to me. I need to have you somewhere in my life. All these other people,' she opened her arms wide to indicate imaginary throngs around her, 'couldn't give a toss about me really. If my career took a dive, they'd be off after the next big thing in a minute. I don't have many friends, actually. Not real ones.' She separated crumbs, setting them out one by one. 'There's Felicity. She's my PA – I guess she's one, although she's more like an older sister,' Blair laughed, 'too much of one sometimes. There's Joanna . . .'

'Joanna who?'

'Joanna Davis.'

'Hang on, I've heard of her. Not for a while, though. What's she doing now?'

'She's not working. Because of something that happened.' Blair paused, and then went on, 'About two years ago this guy began sending her stuff, flowers, letters, cards. And there were phone calls.'

'You mean like a stalker?'

Blair nodded, 'Yes. Like that. It started off small – she thought it was just another fan to start with – some of them can get a bit obsessive. But this guy was off the wall. It got bad. Serious. The things he was sending got worse and worse and then he started threatening her . . .'

'Didn't she do anything about it?'

'Oh, yes. The studio hired bodyguards, security guys, she even moved into a hotel – that's where he got her . . .'

'What happened?'

'He stabbed her.'

'Really?' Louise's blue-grey eyes widened in horror.

'Yes, really. She hasn't worked since.'

'I don't remember reading about that.' Louise frowned.

'You wouldn't. They kept it quiet. A big splash just encourages copycats. They got the guy, and she wasn't very badly hurt, but she was traumatized, you know? She couldn't work – that's how I got the part of Etta, I took Joanna's place on the set of *Born to Kill*. For a while she wouldn't even go out of the house. She's getting better, but it's taken a long time. I try to see her as often as I can.'

Blair's initial visits had been driven by guilt about taking the other actress's part, but now she went out of friendship. She genuinely liked the tall slow-speaking Texan. Hollywood is a cruel place. When your luck fails, so do your friends. Blair did not want to be counted as part of that equation.

'And there's Chris,' she said, recollecting what they had been talking about. 'Chris James. I'd almost forgotten about him. He's another friend, I guess.'

'Who's he?' Louise asked. 'What's he been in?'

Blair laughed. 'He's not famous. He's my personal fitness trainer. He's brilliant. He helped me with *Degrees of Difficulty.* You know, the diving movie? I had to get fit for that, so I went to a gym. That's where I met him. I thought to play the part, really play the part, I needed to know what a diver would do, what a diver would feel. It's not enough just to stand on the platform, posing about in a Speedo, no matter how good you look.'

And Blair looked good. Louise had seen the stills in magazines.

'I wanted to learn to dive. So they got in all these coaches, some of them had worked with the US Olympic team but,' Blair grimaced, 'they were all, like, so boring and technical – I couldn't understand anything they were talking about. They started to say there was no way I was going to learn, which made me *so* angry, then Chris offered to help.' She shrugged. 'And suddenly I could do it. He made it seem easy. And he's from round here too. He was doing a term at an American college as part of his degree course. You'll meet him. He's working at a Health Club, practically next door to the house Gina took. I've been training there.'

'That's a coincidence.'

Blair shrugged. She hadn't thought about it

exactly like that. She was used to everything being the way she wanted.

'Hang on.' Louise's eyes narrowed. 'How am *I* going to meet him?'

'Oh, didn't I say? I've had a great idea. I want you to come and work for me!'

'What?'

'I'm offering you a job. While we're in the UK. A kind of PA. But not like Felicity. You won't have to do any boring stuff. You'd be more like a companion. That's if you want—'

'Yes,' Louise said quickly. 'I want.'

Of all things, she had not expected Blair to come out with that. It would be a dream come true. Being PA to a movie star beat working on a Sainsbury's till.

'It sounds brilliant! When do I start!'

'Right now.' Blair glanced out of the window. 'It's stopped raining – let's go out in the garden.'

They went through the French windows into the dinky little back garden. There had been changes – a paved patio area with table and chairs – but some things were the same.

'You've still got the swings and slide!'

'Oh, I know. Dad keeps saying he's going to get rid of it, but it's still here.'

Blair was delighted. The garden set was still in place, although the bright plastic was faded now, the shiny surfaces roughened and weathered. They wiped the rain off the seats and sat on the swings, hanging side by side.

'Do you remember when we had a competition to see who could go highest and the whole thing almost fell over?' Blair said, pushing backwards and forwards with her foot.

'And you panicked and jumped off and landed in the mud?'

'Yeah, and Gina went mad because I went home filthy.'

She climbed the slide and hung from the top, her lithe body stretching the length of the chute.

'Do you remember when I fell off and cut my leg?' she asked Louise from the top.

'And Gina had a go at my mother, threatened to sue her. Said it was an "unsafe structure".'

'Have you still got the paddling pool?'

'No.' Louise shook her head. 'That went years ago. But do you remember the one in the park? That time you left your knickers there and announced the fact to the whole of W.H. Smith's?'

'Do you remember Gina's face?' Blair was laughing so much the slide began to shake. 'She dragged me off to Marks to buy new ones . . .'

'That was even worse. You insisted on demonstrating exactly why you needed another pair . . .' Louise pulled on her swing again, boosting herself up and back into their shared childhood. 'Do you remember when we bust your Dad's cold frame and blamed it on Stephen? And do you remember when Stephen locked you in the shed and nobody found you until it was nearly dark?'

Blair wiped the tears from her eyes and started

to climb down the slide. Yes. She remembered. He handcuffed her to the bench, locked the door and went off with his friends, leaving her in the dusty dark, alone with the spiders and earwigs. She screamed and cried and nobody heard, nobody came. She remembered and it wasn't funny.

'Have you seen him?' Louise asked. 'Stephen, I mean.'

'Yes. Briefly. Why don't you go and get dressed? Maybe we could go out somewhere.'

Louise jumped off the swing.

'OK. Good idea. I won't be long. Help yourself to coffee.'

Blair did not go into the house, not right away. She walked round the garden. The air was getting warmer. Red hot pokers glowed and the air was heavy with the scent of honeysuckle. She and Louise had practically lived out here in the summer. Her own garden, two doors up, had been almost identical in layout – shed and cold frames at the back – but they almost never played in it. Blair had always preferred this one. Louise's mother liked gardening, took a pride in everything looking nice. Blair never remembered her own mother planting a flower, or touching a rake or trowel. Instead, she had used the straggling uncut lawn and weed-choked borders to fuel her restless dissatisfaction.

Over the fence, she could see the back of her old home, identify her own bedroom. Yellow curtains. Hers had been blue. Another child's collection of soft toys sat in a row on the window sill, just like hers had when she'd lived there with Stephen, Mum and Dad. The family intact. Unlike her mother, Blair remembered the years she had spent here with affection.

She thought of her own garden, back in LA. It would take up most of this housing estate. Irrigation systems swished, keeping it bright and green in the searing heat. Gina didn't do any of it, of course, just lolled by the pool, ordering about an army of Mexican gardeners. The pool was as big as this garden and the next one put together.

Blair let herself back in and closed the patio doors wondering if she would make the swap: her life now, for what might have been. She glanced round the living room. Everything was so small. In Beverley Hills, this wouldn't even be servants' quarters. The house she lived in now, the one Gina had just bought, was vast, the interior designed by one of Gina's friends, but it showed no personal taste, no individuality. There were no presents, no knick-knacks like in Louise's living room. Nothing had been chosen because anyone liked it, but purely because it matched, or was the right thing to have, an investment.

Blair wandered into the hall, glanced at herself in the mirror and then looked down. She rarely admired her own looks. She took them for granted. There was a card propped up against the phone.

Della Rivers *FemTec*
Investigation–Security–Surveillance

- All types of investigation
- Immediate confidential advice
- Discreet service
- Peace of mind
- Highly competitive rates

Blair studied it for a moment before slipping it into her pocket. She walked back towards the kitchen, looking at the pictures in the hall. School photographs smiled back at her. Louise and her brother and sister. Some on their own, others in combination. Blair studied the changing Louise. Her face thinning down, strong features emerging from the puppy fat. Fair hair growing darker, longer, more unkempt. Her smile becoming increasingly enigmatic, the eyes more guarded. Would she swap her life with Louise?

Possibly. Blair loved her fame and success and the wealth and privilege that went with it. At present she was *babe du jour,* girl of the moment, but she knew fame was ephemeral. Hers was a life built on insecurity. It sometimes seemed to Blair that the paparazzi were looking behind her, waiting to see who would be next along. Amongst all the smiling faces, it was difficult to tell who wanted to know you just for yourself.

She thought about Joanna Davis and her hand curled round the card she had just acquired. Perhaps Joanna had prompted her to pick it up. What had happened to her fellow actress could happen to any one of them. It could happen to Blair. There is a very fine line between the adoring fan and the obsessive fanatic. All that adoration fuels darker emotions.

Blair had arrived at premieres, on the arm of some handsome young star, walked up the steps in a $10,000 dress, posed for the flashing cameras: 'Blair! Blair! Over here! Over here, honey!' She had turned, with her escort, to the screaming fans, kept back behind crash barriers by sweating police. She had waved and smiled, feeling the rush of exhilaration. That kind of adulation gave the ultimate high, but it had a downside. Fear was there, like the taste of metal in your mouth. Beneath the glitter and glitz lay a dark shadow, black as midnight. If the barriers gave way, if the police broke ranks, the crowd would surge forward, and they wanted you. Wanted to own you. You were theirs. You belonged to them. They would tear your clothes from your body, your flesh from your bones. Given the chance, they would literally tear you apart . . .

'What's up?' Louise came down the stairs and caught the troubled look on Blair's face. 'Is everything all right?'

'What? Oh, yes – I guess. I was just wondering . . .' She showed Louise the card. 'Are they any good?'

'FemTec? They're the best! I did my work

experience there – it was brilliant. Why?' Louise laughed. 'You're not thinking of hiring them, are you?'

'Maybe.' Blair tapped the card on her chin. Louise had meant it as a joke but she could now see that Blair was serious. 'How about giving them a ring for me?'

'There's no one in,' Louise said. 'I've just phoned.'

'OK.' Blair shrugged and put the card back in her pocket. 'There's no stress. We'll try later. Meanwhile how'd you fancy going to the pictures, to see *Degrees of Difficulty*? You haven't seen it, have you?'

'No.' Louise shook her head. 'It's only just opened here.'

'OK. Let's go.'

Louise picked up her keys and opened the door.

'Where's the car?'

'I made the driver park round the corner.'

'Driver?'

'You know, like chauffeur. What's the matter?' Louise was laughing.

'Nothing. You should have parked outside. You know how they gossip round here. Louise Morgan's chauffeur-driven visitor. Keep the neighbours going for a week.'

Net curtains twitched as the front door slammed. Old Mrs Crompton, in the house opposite, held the thin material and watched them walk out. Louise Morgan, she'd been in all along. She'd told that nice man when he'd rung her bell instead.

'Perhaps the bell isn't working,' she had suggested, 'or she'll be playing music, like that lot next door to me. I thought I saw a friend go in, not so long ago . . .'

'That's all right,' the man had smiled; he had a nice smile. 'Perhaps you can help me?'

Mrs Crompton had been glad to oblige. He'd been enquiring about a friend of his, who used to live at number 25. He'd tried and got no answer. The Morgans had lived at number 25 ever since their Louise was born, Mrs Crompton told him, and she'd be about fifteen, or was it sixteen now? She'd lost track. Her memory wasn't what it used to be, but it was a long time anyhow. She'd advised him to check the address again and, sure enough, it turned out he wanted Melrose Road, not the Crescent. He'd apologized and gone on his way. She didn't mind, it broke up the day. He was such a nice looking chap, so polite. These days people with manners were quite a rarity.

She was still peering out when 'that nice man' drove past, but she did not recognize him. He'd been parked up at the end of the road, baseball cap visor down, collar up, watching number 25. He speeded up to pass the old bag's house, and then slowed down. The girl's Merc was parked up on the main road. He'd followed it from Blair's house. A driver, and all. He smiled to himself. Well, well. This was going to be exciting.

At first he had thought she had just come back on some kind of nostalgia trip, then she'd disappeared into number 25. He had not been able to see who opened the door, but verifying who lived there had been simple. He'd seen the curtains move across the street. He gave Blair a couple of minutes. When it was clear she was staying, he went up and pretended to ring the bell. Then across the street for the information. Louise Morgan. Easy. Now there were two of them. If he missed one, he'd do the other.

He hummed a couple of bars, drumming his fingers to the blues tune, as he watched for the long sleek Mercedes to pull out into the traffic. He turned right, out of the cul-de-sac, and slipped in behind. He saw the driver's eyes slide to his mirror, and dropped a car or two back. He had to be careful. The driver would be experienced, on the lookout, ex-police probably, doubling as a bodyguard, undoubtedly, and that car could outrun this thing any time. It wouldn't do to be spotted now. Not when he was just beginning to enjoy himself.

Chapter 5

Felicity was opening the morning mail. It was her first job of the day. Blair got hundreds of letters every week: fan mail, scripts, publicity material for her approval. Mostly routine things, forwarded by the film company, but two items this morning had attracted her special attention. One was a brown envelope. Could be a bill. Except it had no name, no address. The other item was a package. An A5 jiffy bag. Local postmark. Addressed to Blair, computer-printed label. The packet was bulky, as though it contained several items, all different sizes. Felicity frowned, alarm bells ringing in her head. She had developed a sixth sense for what the Americans term 'inappropriate' correspondence.

'Aren't you going to open it?'

Blair's voice behind her made her jump.

'What are you doing here?' Felicity asked, nonplussed. 'I thought you'd be out jogging, or swimming, or something.'

'Not this morning. I'm going to pick up Louise. What's that?' Blair pointed to the packet. 'A bomb or something?'

'It could be.' Felicity was serious.

'I'll open it.' Blair took it from her. 'It's addressed to me.'

'No!' Felicity shouted.

'Too late!' Blair slit the sealed flap with the

paper knife. 'See? No explosions. Honestly, Flee, you can be so . . . What's this?'

She shook the envelope. The contents dropped onto the table. Blair's hands moved slowly as she sorted through the items, fingers numbing as she separated them out. Her fine jawline tensed and a muscle jumped under her high cheekbone. A ticket for the short stay car park at Heathrow. Room service menu from the hotel where she had stayed in London. Coaster from the bar. A card from a restaurant where she'd had lunch with Bryn. Everywhere she'd been, everything she'd done, someone else had been there too, watching. The remembered times came into her mind and any pleasure in them shrivelled and died.

Felicity opened the other envelope. It contained only one thing. A computer-issued cinema ticket, for *Degrees of Difficulty,* dated yesterday. There was something on the back. Felicity turned it over, feeling slightly sick. There was a message attached, on blue Dynotape:

BESTFILMTODATEIHOPELOUISE
ENJOYEDITASMUCHASIDID!

Blair looked up at Felicity and their eyes met. They didn't have to say anything. They both knew. This was stalker behaviour.

'The reference to Louise . . .'

'Yesterday,' Blair replied, distracted. 'I took her to see it.'

'I'll get on to security . . .'

Felicity reached for the phone.

'Fat lot of use they are!' Blair said, her voice shaking. 'He followed me round all yesterday! Jesus Christ! What was the driver doing? I'm going to handle this myself.' She scooped up the items and put them back in their envelopes. 'Call this number instead.' She gave Della's card to Felicity. 'Make an appointment.'

'What time for?'

'12 o'clock.'

'What shall I tell Gina?'

'Don't tell her anything.' She picked up her PA's car keys from the desk. 'See you, Felicity.'

Chapter 6

SCREEN SCENE

(vol. 2, no. 6 - UK edition)

FACES TO WATCH

Paige, Blair (1978–)

Oscar-nominated at twelve for her riveting performance in THE PHOTOGRAPHER, Paul Green's surprise art-house smash, Blair Paige has proved she can act. Her screen presence and versatility have made this British actress one of Hollywood's favourite children. The question is: where to now? Post-adolescence can be a testing time for a child star.

No stranger to controversy, Blair has ridden the furore surrounding her latest role as Olympic hopeful Clare Morris in Brad Hawkes' DEGREES OF DIFFICULTY with characteristic cool, but let's not kid ourselves, the punters are not flocking in to award her points on her pool entry technique. Dubbed in the press 'Olympic Lolita', DEGREES has made our girl *babe du jour.* We can only hope, for Blair's sake, that the film does not dish out the single trip to oblivion that has been the lot of certain other young stars. As one ex-Lola is quoted as saying: *that film ruined my life!*

REVIEWS
(sources various)

THE PHOTOGRAPHER
1990
109m
Cert. 18
d. Peter Green
OnLine Productions
Brooding study of Victorian photographer Aldo Wyatt

(*Tristan Butler*) and his tortured relationship with enigmatic housekeeper, Mollie (*Elinor Walters*). The story is seen through the eyes and memory of Agnes (*Blair Paige*), her autistic twelve-year-old daughter, the focal point of Wyatt's desire and his obsessive lens. Filmed in sepia/black and white each shot recalls the photographer's life and work. The film is strong on the hypocrisy of Victorian life and hectic decadence of *fin de siècle* London. The gradual movement from seeming normality to moral disintegration is masterly and the tragic inevitability of the film's denouement does not fail to shock.

Former child model *Blair Paige* is impressive in her first big-screen role. Her mixture of grave innocence and nascent self awareness duplicates exactly the 'forbidden fruit' quality of Wyatt's photography. This riveting performance won her a deserved Oscar nomination. Attacked in some sections of the press for allowing her daughter to pose in the nude, Gina Paige fielded accusations of voyeurism, child abuse and pornography. 'There was absolutely *no* exploitation,' insisted Gina. 'Blair was protected every step of the way.' The controversy surrounding the film helped catapult it from art-house movie to blockbuster status.

BORN TO KILL

1995
118m
Cert. 18
d. Monica Clancy
WBFD

Audacious and shocking, this story of a white trash thrill-kill teenage couple's murder spree through the culturally empty spaces and shopping malls of Middle America almost failed to obtain a certificate after being blamed for a series of copycat crimes. More a critique of media values (or lack of them) and moral emptiness than a celebration of violence, BORN TO KILL has nevertheless provoked a firestorm of moral outrage. Late choice *Blair Paige* (last-minute replacement for *Joanna Davis*) is superb as the gum-chewing girlfriend, saturated in media trivia, for whom life is played out on the computer console and video screen. Director *Monica Clancy* neither romanticizes nor condemns, but lets her characters speak for themselves, as *Paige* drags her moronic boyfriend Chas (*Drew Chambers*) on into ever widening circles of destruction.

An impressive directorial debut. Despite the unfortunate loss of *Joanna Davis*, *Blair Paige* proved an inspired choice for the lead.

DEGREES OF DIFFICULTY

1996
124m
Cert. 18
d. Brad Hawkes
Hawkes Production

The surprise hit of the summer. Audiences have flocked to see ex-action hunk Brad Hawkes in his first directorial debut and stayed to watch *Blair Paige*. *Hawkes* plays rugged diving coach Forbes, trainer and mentor to fifteen-year-old debutante diver Clare Morris (*Blair Paige*). The young British actress insisted on performing many of the diving sequences herself. This brings a validity to a performance which looks like taking her way ahead of the pack.

The combination of beauty, guts and courage lends depth and truth to the character of Clare and makes the film's tragic denouement both poignant and inevitable.

DEGREES OF DIFFICULTY contains all the nail-biting tension of the classic sports movie Olympic build-up (Will she? Won't she?) but it is the human story which grips. The doomed relationship between wide-eyed young hopeful and experienced old hand has been done before, but rarely as powerfully as this. The scene where Clare dives naked for Forbes into an eerily lit night-time pool is particularly memorable. Accusations of voyeurism are, in this reviewer's opinion, ill-founded. The movies make voyeurs of us all. If you think this film is obscene – get a life!

• DEGREES OF DIFFICULTY

SYNOPSIS

Experienced College Coach, Forbes takes on young High School hopeful Clare Morris. His experience and her talent promise a guaranteed trip to the Olympics. Their relationship becomes progressively closer and more exclusive until the professional spills into the personal and the two become lovers.

Morris's Olympic hopes are compromised when a jealous rival tips off the press. The story breaks on the final day of competition. The strain proves too much for Morris, robbing her of hoped-for gold. Her sense of failure is reinforced by her coach's reaction. Rejected by him, spurned by her family, in the final desperate scenes she dives from a high-rise building, taking her own life.

Della Rivers read all she could find on Blair Paige. It was important to know as much as possible about prospective clients before they walked into the office. In this case compiling a detailed resumé had not been difficult. Blair's latest film meant that all the magazines had features on her . . .

WHAT'S SO SPECIAL ABOUT... ?

Blair Paige

WE ASKED THOSE IN THE KNOW...

☆

▷ <u>*BLAIR'S MUM, GINA:*</u> I knew she was ***special*** even before she was born. She showed her talent very early on – and hasn't disappointed me yet!

☆

▷ <u>*BRAD HAWKES, DIRECTOR OF DEGREES:*</u> I knew she was different as soon as she walked on the set. She's going to be a ***great actress*** and I've worked with the best!

☆

▷ <u>*EDITOR, SCREEN SCENE, MAX SMITH:*</u> She's a very nice girl, so unpretentious and unspoilt, ***super*** to interview.

☆

▷ <u>*HEAL GAIN, TOP MAKE-UP ARTIST:*</u> Bone structure to die for! But real sweet with it. Patient, unassuming, it's like she doesn't realize how ***beautiful*** she is!

☆

▷ <u>*CELEB SNIPPER, ANDY DEAL:*</u> Blair has ***gorgeous*** hair, so thick and lustrous. All those curls and waves make it a dream to style.

☆

▷ <u>*LISA JONES, JOURNALIST:*</u> I was completely won over by her ***charm*** and enthusiasm. I went in expecting a movie brat and came out feeling I'd met a major talent.

☆

▷ <u>*MORAG O'DONNELL, DIRECTOR:*</u> Blair can appear both ***sophisticated*** and naive, mature but childlike at the same time. This brings a unique quality to her acting.

☆

▷ BILL NICHOLLS, TOP SNAPPER: Being so **famous** and gorgeous, could make her a bit of a prima donna. Not at all! Blair's a dream to work with!

☆ And finally... ☆

BLAIR ON BLAIR

“ *'...I don't think I'm special at all. Just lucky, that's all...'* ”

'...I haven't met any guy that I'd want to get serious about. Friends are more important at the moment...' “

'...all this stuff about my body, my looks, it really ticks me off. I just want to be taken seriously, as an actress...' ”

'...mature for my age? Yes, I guess I am. I try to be as normal as I can, but I don't know about the average teenager's life 'cos my life has not been average...' ”

'...fame? Who knows haw long it will last? I never take anything for granted...' ”

These quotes were pre-selected, but they showed a girl popular with her fellow professionals. A star who had charmed quite a few journalists with her refreshing lack of conceit.

Della sat forward in her chair, chin resting on her hands, contemplating stills of Blair from her different films. She really was a beautiful girl. Her beauty lay in her eyes, huge and violet blue under finely arched brows, and the proportions of her face. A slight widening of the jaw balanced the full mouth and added depth to the high cheekbones. Her face was young, but she could project any mood the photographers threw at her, from wide-eyed innocence to sultry seduction. But that was just her face. Della tore herself away from the physical image, and turned back to the interviews.

Blair handled questions about the controversial nature of her roles with disarming frankness, and did not seem in the least fazed by the media furore surrounding her latest: *Degrees of Difficulty*. She was especially complimentary about her male co-star/director, who played the coach, attributing the film's success to his name, his performance both as actor and director. She had less to say about her own part in the film's success, and yet, for the part, she had learned to dive. Della shook her head. Diving took guts and courage, as well as gymnastic ability. Blair clearly took her acting very seriously, but that was not something she chose to discuss at length.

She did not come over as quite so in charge when handling questions about herself. The interviews all noticeably lacked biographical detail. She carried her public fame well, but she was far less forthcoming about her private life. She either turned it back on the interviewer (Who do *you* date? What was *your* idea of a good time?) or refused to answer. She was even less open about her family. She had a brother, Stephen, older than her, living in Britain, training to be a doctor. What did he think of his sister's films? You'd have to ask him that. How did he feel about having such a famous sister? No comment. As for her father, there was no mention of him at all; he seemed to have dropped off the planet.

Gina Paige seemed to be her only real family. Her mother's role in her climb to fame and fortune was widely acknowledged, taken as read, but their actual relationship? That was a different matter. Gina Paige often sat in, and one interviewer was practically thrown out for digging under the surface. The journalist had turned her questioning in Gina's direction. Asking if, as a mother, she was happy for her daughter to appear in a film (*Degrees of Difficulty*) which showed her in a sexual relationship with a middle-aged man. Never mind that it wasn't really Blair up there in bed, wasn't it kind of disturbing? For Blair herself, let alone all the men out there, watching a young girl . . . *Interview terminated.*

Questions about *The Photographer* had met with the same response. Della flicked back to the film reviews. Blair was only twelve when she made that. One of the film magazines contained part of an interview made just after the Oscar nomination. The shots of Blair posing, nude, or semi-nude, the interviewer asked, a tad voyeuristic, wouldn't you say? Certainly not! came Gina's response. It was artistic. Blair was protected every step of the way. But what does that *mean*, Mrs Paige? How did Blair herself feel about it? Blair did not give interviews back then, but she felt fine, just fine. We have her mother's word for it.

Della frowned and checked her watch. 11.45. Blair's 'people' had made contact earlier in the morning to make a noon appointment. Wendy Miller, the senior partner and FemTec founder, had taken the call. She was giving evidence in court for most of the day and had handed the case to Della. Her junior partner had a couple of questions, like how on earth had an international star like Blair Paige heard of their firm? Looked them up in Yellow Pages? And why them? She could hire a big outfit, like Belmont. Wendy had dismissed Della's doubts. They were lucky to win a prestige contract – who cared how they got it? She had left for court telling Della to put her kid gloves on. Della swung in her chair, drumming her long fingers on the arms, annoyed with herself for feeling nervous.

'She's expecting a client, but they ain't due for a bit.' Janine's local accent sang in from the outer office. 'Nah, she won't mind if you make it quick.'

Della sighed with impatience. She had left

strict instructions not to be disturbed. Whoever it was had better be someone she wanted to see and they had better make it snappy.

Two young women entered. She recognized one of them.

'Louise! Hi! Oh, God.' Della put her hand to her forehead. 'I clean forgot to return your call. I'm sorry. Could have saved you the journey. Nothing doing, I'm afraid. Summer's a bad time. Everyone's on holiday. Even criminals take a break.'

'Della,' Louise started to say, 'this is . . .'

But Della cut her off. 'To tell you the truth, now is not a good time. I'm expecting a client. Personally, I think it's a wind-up but Wendy is taking it seriously. I don't want to be rude or anything, but . . .'

Blair was watching Della from under her hat. The detective was leaning back in her chair, one foot resting on the edge of the desk. Nice boots. Thin soled, glove-soft leather. Expensive. So was the suit. Well cut, charcoal grey with a chalk stripe, double-breasted waistcoat, wide trousers with turn-ups. The jacket cuffs, folded back, revealed a white cufflinked shirt, bony wrists, and a chunky metal watch, possibly a Rolex. Della was tall and slim. Her clothes seemed to fold round her long legs and arms. Her face was angular. Wide mouth, aquiline nose, high cheek-bones. Short dark hair, well cut, feathered into points which framed her face and went some way to relieve the severity of her features. She wore three earrings, all different. A stud and a gold hoop in her right ear, a dropper in the other. Jet or onyx, it was hard to see. Ought to be aquamarine to go with her eyes. They really were most extraordinary. A light, clear green. Blair, wondering if she might be wearing colour contacts, moved to get a better view, and found them staring right into her own.

'Would your friend mind stepping forward and removing her hat?' Della said to Louise.

Blair did as she was told.

Della glanced down at her desk, then back at Blair and laughed.

'Blair Paige, I believe . . .'

How had Blair Paige heard of them? Answer: Louise Morgan. They knew each other from way back. Della had forgotten. *Some detective I am,* she thought, inviting the girls to sit down.

The building they were in was a three-storey low-rise office block. Red brick and glass, blue-painted window frames and portico, 1980s modern but tasteful, designed to fit in with, even complement, the tall Edwardian town houses which made up the rest of the row. These were mostly offices also. Solicitors, accountants, insurance brokers. His high-powered compact binoculars could pick out names on the furthest brass plaque, but he turned his attention to the building in front of him. They had gone to the third floor. He had watched them ascend the glassed-in staircase which ran up the centre of the building. He fine-focused the binoculars, bringing up individual firms, but the signs did not show which floor or the nature of the work they were engaged in. He grabbed the clipboard he kept in the dash drawer and ran across the road, up the steps, and knocked on the half-open door of the first office on the left, Kendall Pensions and Life.

'Excuse me, love. Wonder if you could help?'

The young woman looked up from her computer screen.

'I work for a market research company . . .' he flashed an ID card, one of several he had acquired, 'and we're doing a survey of the occupation patterns in small business premises in quasi-residential areas . . .'

He looked over his board, assessing the impact so far. The more boring the chat, the quicker the result.

'How can I help?'

Worked every time. He smiled. The girl smiled back.

'I've been up that many stairs, Mandy.' He read her name off the label on her desk. 'You don't mind me calling you Mandy, do you?'

She shook her head, not at all. It was a change to see a friendly face. Mr Bishop, her boss, hardly said two words to her and Pensions and Life Assurance didn't get that many interesting visitors.

'You couldn't tell me who else is in this building?'

'Sure.'

She began to rattle them off. He bent his dark head over the clipboard, pretending to have trouble keeping up.

' . . . and on the third floor, Anderson Floyd, they're brokers, Richmond and Hardy, property consultants, and FemTec.'

'Who are they?'

'Investigations and surveillance.' She dropped her voice, to emphasize the secrecy and importance of their work. 'Really it's a detective agency.'

'FemTec . . .'

He'd written the name down once from the sign outside but he wrote it down again, for effect. His heart beat harder in his chest; that's where they had been going.

'Funny name,' he added, wondering what more he might be able to find out.

The girl giggled.

'Isn't it? Della hates it. It was Wendy's idea and she's senior partner. She's in court today, giving evidence,' she added, her voice taking that hushed tone again. 'I met her on her way out this morning.'

'Who's Della?'

The question came out casually.

'Della Rivers? She's the other partner. It's all women, you see.'

'All women, what?'

'An all-women agency. They don't have any male operatives.'

'You're kidding me! Like those two on the telly?'

'Yes, kind of. Most of their clients are women so it makes sense. I mean, if it was me . . .'

He wrote *Della Rivers* quickly, circling the name, while she went on to explain what she would require if she were to employ a detective agency.

'I was just about to make a coffee, do you fancy a cup?'

'No, I won't, if you don't mind. I've kept you long enough and I'd better be getting on myself.' He gave her a cheery wave from the door. 'Thanks a lot, Mandy. You've been a great help.'

'Who was that?' A voice shouted from the inner office.

'Nobody, Mr Bishop.'

'Any chance of a coffee?'

'Just making one. Be ready in a minute.'

Mandy sighed as she dropped in the coffee granules and watched them dissolve under the stream of boiling water. Pity that guy couldn't have stayed for a while. There was no one to chat to here and he'd been nice. She wished everyone who came in was as nice as that.

He drove round the block and into the same street, finding a convenient parking spot, well back from Mandy and her vertical slatted blinds but still within sight of the entrance.

Chapter 7

Della surveyed the items Blair had given to her. Small, ordinary, everyday things that anyone might pick up and keep in a handbag or wallet. Things which said, 'This is where I've been, this is what I did', but these carried a different message. They said, simple and strong: 'I'm watching you, I know where you are, I know what you do.' It was a neat idea and so much better than a letter. Handwriting could be analysed and compared. Letters could get lost in the hundreds that came every week, shunted off to a fan club, read and intercepted. Blair was right to be worried. This was not some besotted fan pouring his heart out, this was stalker behaviour.

'You received these today?' Della studied the envelope.

Blair nodded. 'It's addressed to Portland House. The place I'm staying at the moment. Even Louise didn't know where I was,' she glanced across at her friend, 'until yesterday. I'm supposed to be in retreat. It is supposed to be secret.'

'What kind of security does the house have?'

'Electronic gates. Guards, alarms, cameras . . .' Blair shrugged, 'you name it.'

'The house has big grounds, presumably. Are they patrolled? You know, with guard dogs?'

'I don't think so.' Blair shrugged. 'I haven't seen any.'

'Name of the firm?'

'I haven't got the slightest idea.' Blair did not concern herself with details like this. 'You'd have to ask Felicity, my PA. They wear blue uniforms, if that's any good . . .'

Della sighed. Didn't they all? Easy enough to check.

'What about this?' Della picked up the ticket by the corners. 'Hand delivered?'

Blair nodded again. 'Seems so.'

'This reference to Louise . . .'

Someone like Blair could expect to attract this kind of attention, but what about Louise? Louise was just an ordinary girl. Della frowned, her eyes narrowing as she re-read the message; that was bad.

'We went to see the movie together yesterday. He must have been right there, in the cinema . . .'

'OK, I agree that this could indicate a stalker, but I still don't understand about the flowers. They were hand-delivered, also?'

Blair nodded.

'Right.' Della leaned forward, massaging her forehead. 'Explain to me again about this Leonora Quinn business.'

'She came to do a reading. Tarot cards.'

'I thought she was an astrologer?'

'She does readings for special clients.'

'At your house?'

'Yes.'

Della raised an eyebrow. One of the biogs said that Blair was into astrology, but Leonora Quinn was nationally known, syndicated, with hotlines; it would take serious money to pull her in for a home session. Blair seemed all right, on the surface, but Della was reserving judgement. Interest in the occult could equal 'unstable'; and having that kind of money, especially so young, made her different from other people.

'How did it go?' she asked, careful not to sound sceptical.

Blair frowned. 'Not well. She didn't come up with anything much. Just kind of boring stuff, but afterwards, when we went downstairs, Felicity, or someone, had put these flowers on the table in the hall. Leonora went over to check her hair, whatever, and she comes reeling back, looking like she's about to pass out. I ask, "What's wrong?" but she just looks at me and says, "Those flowers. Get them out of the house." '

'I see. And that's it? She didn't say anything else? Maybe she's allergic . . .'

Blair shook her head vehemently. 'She told me that if they were not removed the evil would spread. She felt a presence, something evil.'

'I see. And these?' Della said, pointing to the paper archive of Blair's life. 'You think the same, er, malevolent presence might be at work here?'

'Don't you?' Blair's blue eyes flared. She expected deference from aides or employees. The detective's scepticism irritated her. 'I need you to take this seriously. Or . . .'

'Or you'll find someone who will?'

'Exactly.'

Della leaned back in her chair.

'I am taking it seriously. Who has access to the house?'

'Me, Felicity, Gina,' Blair counted them off, 'my brother, Stephen, and Chris James, my personal trainer.'

Della wrote the last two names down.

'OK. Let's take Stephen. Does he live locally?'

'Yes. Just a few miles from here, as a matter of fact. He's studying medicine at Mercia.'

She glanced out of the window. You could see the university tower from Della's Edgely office.

'How often have you seen him? Since you got back?'

'He met us. Stayed a couple of days in London . . .'

'Has he been to the house?'

'Once or twice. He's got his own life—'

'Have you visited him?'

'No.'

'OK. Apart from now – the last time you saw him was?'

'About a year ago. Why?'

'How would you describe your relationship with him. Close?'

'Yes, I guess . . .'

'How about him and your mother?'

'They . . .' Blair stalled. 'Why are you asking all this?'

'Because I need to know.' Della did not look up from her notes. 'OK. He's at the airport to meet you, he's with you in London for a few days, and you were there what? A week, two?'

'More like three.'

'And since then you've hardly seen him? That about it?'

'Yes, but I don't see . . .'

'Right.' Della drew a line under her notes on Stephen. 'What about this other guy? Chris James. Tell me about him.'

'He's my personal trainer. We worked together in LA. He helped me with the diving in *Degrees*, you know, the film . . .'

'And . . .?'

'That's it.'

'That's not it, Blair. How come he's here? Working with you now?'

Blair relaxed a little. That was easy.

'He comes from round here. When I knew we were coming over I got in touch. He's working at The Greswoldes—'

'The health hydro place?'

'Yes. You know it?'

Della nodded. It was frequented by media types and the local wealthy. Very exclusive.

'It's right next to Portland House.'

'Handy.'

'Yes. Isn't it?'

'How did he get a job there?

'Well, he's very good and I suggested it, I guess.'

'How did you do that?'

'Part of the deal on the house we are renting.

The Greswoldes is owned by the same consortium.'

'Right. You must have wanted him a lot, then. To get him a job, and all?'

'Like I said, he's very good . . .'

'Is that the only reason?'

'Of course. What other reason could there be? Hey – if you're implying that there's anything between Chris and me . . .'

'I'm not implying anything. Is there?'

'No!'

'Has there been?'

'No again.' Blair shook her head vehemently. 'I don't like this line of questioning.'

'All right. Try this. How old is he? Chris, I mean?'

'I don't know, mid-twenties . . .'

'How does he feel about a teenage girl getting him a job?'

'I don't know.' Blair was really annoyed now, lines of colour washing her high cheekbones. 'You'd have to ask him.'

'OK. Calm down.' Della smiled. 'I'm not a journalist, you know. I'm a detective. I'm just trying to get an idea of the people around you. Those who can get close to you. Some of the items have been hand-delivered.' She laced her fingers under her chin. 'Everything you tell me is absolutely confidential. Do you want me to help you or not?'

'OK. OK. I'm sorry. Yes. I do.'

'All right. Consider me hired.' Della stood up

and shook Blair's hand again. 'Just one more thing – does your mother know – I mean about this arrangement . . .?'

Blair's smile froze. 'It's my money, Della. I earned it, not my mother. So I choose what to do with it and how to spend it. Is that clear?'

'Absolutely. Nice doing business with you.'

Della went to the window to watch them go. He had more than likely followed Blair, but Della saw no one obviously tailing the distinctive red car. That did not mean he wasn't there – it just meant he could not be seen. She stood looking down through the slatted blinds. Cars parked both sides despite double yellow lines. Pedestrians taking a short cut to the shops; office workers on their lunch break. It was so easy to hide by being one of the throng, just another car in the constant flow of traffic. Modern city life allows stalkers to do the impossible: render themselves invisible.

Della stayed at the window, going over what she knew about stalkers. They are hard to categorize, taking in all kinds, from all walks of life. Ages vary from teenager to pensioner. Only a few are dangerous, but all are capable of making the subject's life a nightmare by sheer persistence.

They divide into two sorts: ones who want the victim to know who they are, and ones, like this guy, who prefer to remain hidden. Della sighed and turned back to her office. Facts and figures might aid understanding but they wouldn't find him. That had to be done by detective work.

She went to her desk and sorted through the items Blair had given her. No handwriting. The message on the ticket was Dynoprinted. Why send them in separate packages? Why post one and then risk hand delivery? Della wrote down the questions and moved the ticket away from the other items.

Finger prints could probably be lifted from the envelopes, maybe, and some of the glossier surfaces. If she was still in the force, she could have it dusted. But she wasn't, and he probably wore gloves. Even if he didn't, it wouldn't count for much unless he was on record. He could be, in all outward respects, an ordinary guy, a law-abiding citizen. She kept saying 'he' all the time. It could be a woman. It was usually men, but around fifteen per cent were women. She had to keep an open mind.

Even if she was in the police, even if she had not resigned one step ahead of disciplinary proceedings, she would not be able to do anything much. Yet. He/she would have to do more than send a girl flowers, and odd things through the post, for the police to be able to act. It did not matter whether the recipient was Blair Paige Movie Star or Little Miss Nobody. Della considered the options. The laws against stalking were getting tougher all the time, but the police had to know who the person was before they could take any course of action, that was the bottom line.

Della wrote a few more notes and then put

down her pen. People think stalking is about love, but it is not. It is not about hatred, either. Stalking is about power, using fear to gain power over another person. She picked up the picture of Blair again. Young, beautiful, rich and successful. To strike fear into her, forcing a way into her life, getting to control her mood, dictate her every move. That was power all right, a stalker would really get off on that.

'What do you think?' Janine came in, interrupting her thoughts.

'Umm, about what?'

'Blair Paige! This case! What did she want?'

'I don't want you talking to anyone about her visit, Janine. Not a word. Understood?'

Janine nodded.

'She wants security,' Della added, softening her tone slightly. 'She's being bothered by someone sending her stuff.' She pointed to the items Blair had given her. 'She's getting some unwanted attention and she wants to discover who's behind it. It's our job to find out for her and, at the same time, protect her confidentiality.'

Della stirred the glossies in front of her. This person was a collector, would clip the pages from the same magazines. It was important to get into the stalker's head. Try to think the same way. But why Blair? Why choose her?

'What are you doing tonight?'

'Nothing,' Janine replied, mystified. 'Why?'

'Fancy going to the pictures?'

'Who with? What to see?'

'*Degrees of Difficulty.*' Della smiled. 'You and me. How about it?'

'Oh, Della.' Janine grinned back. 'I thought you'd never ask!'

'Your family don't mind, do they? Me dragging you away like this?' Blair asked as they turned in to Portland House.

'Of course not,' Louise replied. 'They're really pleased for me. Dad's a bit worried. Thinks it will turn my head. I'll never settle back into an ordinary existence. Only kidding—'

'Stephen's back. That's his car!'

Blair accelerated down the rest of the drive and skidded to a halt next to a black VW GTi.

Stephen was standing in the hall. Blair rushed to her brother, throwing her arms round him. He lifted her up off the ground and kissed her. Lightly on the mouth. Eyes closed, his lashes as long and dark as Blair's own.

The caress lasted a fraction too long and seemed too intimate, wrong between brother and sister. Louise turned away, surprised by her own reaction and then looked back, annoyed with herself for being so conventional.

'Is it OK if I stay for a while?' he said.

'Of course. You don't have to ask.'

They stood looking at each other for a moment, then Blair, still holding his hand, brought him over to meet Louise.

'Steve, this is Louise. Louise Morgan.'

Louise remembered him from the time when they had lived in the same street. He didn't play with them, boys and girls of different ages rarely mixing, but she remembered him well. He and Blair had looked almost like twins then, but the years had brought differences. He had the same silky dark hair and blue eyes but his features were less well balanced, more heavily defined, as though a sculptor, setting out to make repeat model of Blair, had been forced to use a coarser clay. He was good-looking, though, there was no denying that.

'How do you do?' he said, taking her hand. 'You've changed a bit since I last saw you.'

'So have you.'

'How long can you stay?' Blair asked, linking their arms.

'As long as you'll have me. Penny's thrown me out,' he said with a wry grin. 'Sleeping on floors is doing my back in.'

'Stephen?' his mother called from the sitting room door. 'Darling! How wonderful!'

Louise hadn't seen Gina for a while. At first glance, she seemed younger. Her ivory linen suit emphasized her slenderness and set off the skin tones achieved through a beautician's skill. Her hair was elaborately dressed like a halo of spun gold candyfloss.

'You can't imagine how pleased I am . . .' she cooed, reaching up to kiss her son.

'And Louise. So glad you could come.' Her smile thinned to a scarlet line. Close up, tiny lines betrayed her age, and her eyes were hard and steely bright behind the subtly blended kohl and fringed mascara. 'It means so much to Blair . . .'

She turned, dismissing the girl, focusing all her attention on to her son and daughter.

Chapter 8

Della arrived early the next morning, parking her car on the road. From the front, Portland House had high stone walls and electronically operated wrought-iron gates but at the back the landscaped garden gave on to dense woodland. Della walked along the grass verge until she came to a stile where yellow arrows marked a public footpath. She climbed over and followed the path into the trees. The surface was muddy and, judging from the prints, was used by joggers and ramblers. Della trod on a stick. It went off like a gun shot. Across from the house first one dog barked, and then another.

From the woods there was a clear view up to the rear of the house. Early-morning sun mellowed the stone from honey to gold. Above the long windows of the large mullioned bay at the back, smaller panes reflected the light this way and that in kaleidoscope diamonds of mirror and black.

A tall young man in uniform was crossing to the bottom of the close-cropped lawn. He had two dogs, Dobermans, on a short leash. Della was too far away to see the badge, but thought it might be Belmont. Dog patrols marked a step-up in security. That was good. Della made her way back to the road. Someone else was taking this threat to Blair seriously.

*

'Ms Rivers. I'm so glad you're here. Blair told me to expect you. I'm Felicity, Blair's PA . . .'

Gina Paige came out of the drawing room, curious to know who was calling at this hour, anxious to know their business.

'Gina Paige,' she introduced herself to the tall young woman in a long white mac. 'Blair's mother. And you are?'

'Della Rivers,' Della said before the PA could intervene. 'Private detective.'

Della gave her a card and followed Felicity to the office.

Gina went up the stairs, to Blair's bedroom, her lips clamped together, rigid with anger. What could Blair be thinking of? Acting on her own. Hiring a private detective. Going behind her mother's back. There was no need for her to interfere. Bryn, Blair's agent and Gina's personal friend, had it all in hand; he was sending somebody up from London.

'I don't want them. I want her.' Blair was sitting on the bed. She did not look up from tying her trainers, but her fine eyebrows were drawn together and her voice became ominously quiet. 'I've had it with guys in suits. I'm the one who pays so I get to choose.' She stood up, lycra shorts and leotard showing off her athletic build. 'Thank you for telling me she's here. I need to speak to her before I take Louise to the health club. I don't want to be late, so if you'll excuse me . . .'

Gina followed her daughter down the stairs, still protesting, but Blair ignored her.

'Della! Thanks for coming!' was all she heard, then Blair closed the door to Felicity's office.

A driver took them to The Greswoldes Health Farm and Country Club, although it was practically next door to Portland House. The Greswoldes had once been a large country house and had kept its imposing porticoed facade but the back had been built to accommodate all the facilities it now provided. Louise had never been anywhere like this before and, as she accompanied Blair across the courtyard, her apprehension was verging on panic. She wasn't exactly fat, but she wasn't exactly thin, either, and this was about to be exposed to Blair – to the whole world. However much she might kid herself, walking to and from the bus stop every day didn't exactly amount to an all-round workout. Blair telling her how exclusive the place was had made her feel worse, not better.

'It's all right for you, but I won't know what to do,' she said, scuffing at the freshly raked gravel, 'and I haven't got any kit. I'll never get into anything of yours . . .'

'Don't worry. You'll be fine,' Blair replied. 'Won't she, Chris? Louise, I'd like you to meet Chris James . . .'

Louise nearly walked into him. She looked up to meet a pair of large dark brown eyes smiling down at her.

'I told you about Chris, didn't I?' Blair smiled slightly. 'He's the best.'

Louise had been looking forward to meeting this man; now she regarded him with even more interest. Blair's tone was quiet, almost shy, and her own standards were so high she rarely praised excellence in other people.

'Hey!' He ducked his head, laughing, shying away from the compliment. 'Don't listen to her. Nice to meet you, Louise. Have you come to work out or just to look round . . .?'

'Oh, well . . .' Louise began, sensing an escape route.

'She's here to work out,' Blair said, as they walked through the doors. 'I'm going to treat her to a whole new outfit, then you can sort out a programme to give her a whole new body.'

Louise sat in the foyer, waiting for Blair to sign her in, watching the traffic of clients and staff. The staff all wore uniforms, coded to describe their function. Those involved with the health side of things wore short white tunics like dental nurses; the fitness staff wore pale grey tracksuits, like the one Chris James wore, with the club's logo on the back. The staff seemed pleasant and helpful, their attention designed to make the clients feel good. Louise looked in the brochure, noting the membership rate and joining fee; that kind of money buys you a great deal of feeling special.

'Louise? Hi, I'm Helen.' A pretty girl with short blonde hair was smiling down at her. 'I understand you want to see our sports boutique? This way. Ms Paige said to meet her there.'

It was unreal. As though she'd won a competition. She could have anything, top of the range trainers, all the best labels. She didn't have to pay for any of it herself, everything was to be charged to her friend's account. All she had to do was try it on. Blair and Helen went from rack to rack, deciding what was needed.

'Leave it on,' she said, as Louise began to struggle out of the kit she was trying. 'We'll just cut the price tags off. Now what do you think, Helen? Nikes or Reeboks? Fives?'

Louise nodded. They went out to select training shoes, socks, tracksuit, bag to put it all in, and don't forget the swimsuit. How much was it going to cost? Louise eyed the swinging labels and decided not to look. She came out of the changing room in her new outfit and stood, wondering how long it would take to get used to having this kind of money, as the till beeped and an assistant gunned the bar codes.

Louise's clothes-inspired confidence began to drain as they entered the gymnasium. Pop music blared out. Mirrored walls reflected a formidable array of exercise machinery. Everyone wore the right gear. No ill-fitting shorts or tatty old T-shirts here. Louise was relieved to see that most of the clients, labouring away with varying degrees of effort and concentration, had not all reached a state of physical perfection; but they were guided and supervised by young men and women, all dressed the same in green vests and black lycra, who wore their perfect fitness like a second corporate logo.

Helen turned to the dark pretty girl on the desk. The staff had name badges; hers read *Adele*.

'Can you tell Chris? Blair is here now.'

Chris James was obviously an exception to the dress code. A wide weightlifter's belt secured baggy grey shorts and the letters were barely readable on his bleached-out LAKERS vest. He was not bodybuilder-huge or overdeveloped. In fact, his body appeared quite normal, until one looked at it closely, and then one could see each muscle defined and outlined, even down to the striations and veins crossing under the smooth sheath of his brown skin. He smiled and Louise shifted her gaze away from him aware that maybe she shouldn't be looking that closely.

'Hi there, Louise. Well, you certainly look the part. Done much exercise before?'

His eyes appraised her body, but not in the usual way, more as if she was an animal and he was assessing her potential.

'You've got a good basis to work from. Helen will take you through our fitness check. Then I'll sort you out a programme.'

'Thank you,' she heard herself say, although she was not exactly sure what for.

'My pleasure.' His smile widened but he was already turning away from her. 'Now Blair, are you ready?'

'You a friend of hers?' Helen said as she adjusted the dials on the exercise bike.

'I've known her for years, ever since we were little kids. There's no need to sound so surprised,' Louise replied, fitting her feet into the pedals.

Helen laughed. 'I'm sorry. I didn't mean to offend you. Keep up a steady pace, that's it. I admire her. Lots of the girls here do. I mean, she really works on that body of hers. I suppose she has to, what with all those nude scenes and close-ups, and everything, especially her latest, *Degrees of Difficulty*. Have you seen it?'

Louise nodded.

'Me too. I thought it was brilliant. All that diving. Did she really learn it just for the film?'

Louise nodded again. Her breath was coming shorter now. The pedalling was beginning to get to her.

'To play an Olympic athlete! And she really looked the part.' Helen shook her head. 'It takes some doing. I bet people don't realize, all the fans and that, I bet they don't realize how hard you have to work if you want to look like that.'

Blair was stripped off now, down to her leotard. 'Slender strength', 'electrifying androgynous grace', magazine phrases came to mind as she went through her stretching exercises. She finished and stood, arms folded, with Chris James close by her side. She was listening, head inclined towards him. As he talked to her, his hand massaged the muscle between her neck and shoulder.

'Keep up the pace, Louise.'

'What?'

'You were slackening off. You've got to keep at it for five minutes steady.'

'Not bad. Not bad at all.'

Chris commented as he read Helen's report. Louise felt like she was back at school.

'Now some of these look pretty intimidating,' he said as he led her over to the clusters of gleaming machinery. 'Don't be put off, they're not, believe me.' He wiped his face and towelled his dark hair. 'It's getting too hot in here. They need to turn up the air conditioning. Last week we had the heating on. I can't stand British weather. Cold one minute, hot the next. Drives me crazy. At least you know where you are in California. I did a semester at UCLA, as part of my degree,' he added as he adjusted the weights behind the first machine.

'Why don't you go back?' Louise asked as she put her arms in the places he showed her.

He laughed, a quick sharp bark. 'I'm not a movie star. I'd need a work permit and, out there, guys like me are two a penny. OK. Squeeze your arms together. That's it. A bit more slowly. I've put it on ten pounds weight and I want fifteen reps. The secret is a little more each time, gradual increase.'

They went on to the next station.

'Now this is for the leg muscles,' he explained. 'You sit here and put your feet under that bit there. Don't start yet! I've got to adjust the weights. Always check them first. There might have been some big guy on it before you and then you'd strain yourself.'

'How long have you been working here?' Louise asked as she lifted the weighted bar up and down.

'Not long, started last month. It's not really my thing, to be honest. Too many rich bored housewives killing time, and overweight businessmen trying to be Schwarzenegger. I prefer to train sports people but,' he shrugged, 'beggars can't be choosers. I'd just finished my degree, no job, living with my dad, then out of the blue, I get an offer from this place. At first I couldn't figure it. And then I realized,' he looked over to Blair in the weights area, 'it was down to her. She made employing me a condition of her joining.'

'That's quite a compliment.'

'Is it?' His brown eyes were on her again and this time they weren't smiling. 'Depends how you look at it. Enough talking, time to get to work.'

He led her to a multigym complex and told her to sit.

'This machine is for the trapezius. This muscle group here.' He touched her lightly across the shoulders. 'Take the bar and pull it down. No. Behind the head. That's it. Fifteen reps.'

The next contraption exercised the inner thighs. Louise sat legs clamped wide apart.

'Squeeze 'em together. That's it,' Chris James laughed. 'Not very dignified, but very effective.'

They went through triceps, biceps, obliques and abdominals. Each station was designed to exercise a different muscle group, and at each one he explained what the machine was for and exactly what to do. Louise listened, following his instructions, and found herself wondering about him, studying him, to take her mind off the ache in her muscles. His dark skin went with his hair and eyes and suited his taut hawk-like features. A face like his could look hard, even severe, but his expression softened when he smiled, which he did often. He had a way of making you feel he was smiling just for you, exclusively, which made you work harder, want to please him. That kind of charm must be useful in his kind of job.

'Can I have a go at what Blair's doing?' she asked as he fitted her into yet another exercise device.

'What?'

She pointed to the weights area. Blair was the only woman there. Groups of men stood around talking or lifting. It was the only part of the gym where the clients looked seriously fit.

Blair lay stretched out on a bench. A young man stood over her, attaching new weights to a bar on a stand above her. He stood back as Blair reached up and lifted the weight off the stand and then stepped forward again to take the strain.

'Oh, no. That's too advanced for you. You'd

have to build your upper body strength considerably.'

'Blair seems to find it easy enough.'

'Blair? She's a natural. Could have been an athlete, if she hadn't taken up acting. Any sport, you name it, up to the highest level. She picked up diving, just like that.' He snapped his fingers. 'And it's not easy, believe me. Not that weights take any skill, just strength and determination.'

'What's he doing? The guy with her.'

'Phil? He's spotting for her. Making sure the bar with the weights doesn't smash down onto her face.' Chris rubbed at a sudden ripple of goose flesh on his arms. 'That'd be a waste. Not to say expensive. Her film company would sue the pants off this place.' He laughed, touching the skin at the side of his mouth, as though smoothing a remembered moustache. 'I'd better take over. Phil looks like it's all getting a bit too much.'

The young man was staring down at Blair's lithe body and long perfectly muscled legs stretched out in front of him. Her hair, coiled and damp, was touching his knees. Sweat stood out on his pale face. He wiped at it with his sleeve to make sure no drips fell onto her from his chin.

'This is your programme, Louise. Give it to Adele. See you next time . . .'

Chris went back to the weights area and took Phil's place, standing over Blair, talking down to her. Louise was having a problem working out how old he was. Usually pretty good on ages, she found it hard to place him. He could have been anything from mid-twenties to thirtysomething. Maybe it was his punishing training regime, or his naturally dark skin, or maybe he was just one of those men who lose the smoothness of youth early but then do not change much until middle age or beyond.

'Aren't we going to get changed, have a shower or something?' Louise said as they left the gym.

'I never change here. I always change at home.'

'Why?'

'I don't like people staring at me. I'm shy about it. What are you laughing at?

'Shy? How can you be shy? You've been strolling around all morning in next to nothing . . .'

'I had a leotard and leggings on.'

'But your body's displayed all over the place, twenty foot high in every multi-screen – every person in the country has probably seen it.'

'You don't understand,' Blair said as they went down the stairs. 'That's not me up there. It's Clare or Etta, or Agnes, or whoever I'm playing. It's not my body they see, it's hers. When it is me, I want some privacy. That's why.'

'Excuse me, Ms Paige?'

They were halfway across the reception area. Blair turned to the young man who had touched her on the shoulder. She saw by his clothes that he was an employee and then she recognized him. He had taken over when Chris had gone to help Louise.

'I didn't like to ask back there, but could I trouble you for your autograph?'

'Sure. But I haven't got a pen.'

'Here.' He produced one from his zip-up top then patted his pockets for paper.

'I'll write on this.' Blair swept up a brochure from a nearby table. 'Do you want it to anyone special?'

'To Philip, please.'

'That's you, right? I remember your name now. 'To Philip. Thanks for spotting for me. Lots of love, Blair.' That do?'

'Yes.' He looked at the paper, then at Blair, as though he couldn't believe what he was seeing. 'That's wonderful.'

A rustle of voices seemed to spread around them.

'It's her. Blair Paige. I thought so.'

'She's the one in that new film.

'The one all the fuss is about?'

'I knew it was her.'

'It is. I'm sure.'

It was the start of a feeding frenzy. Blair was besieged by nearly every person in the foyer, all asking for autographs. For themselves, for sons and daughters, nieces and nephews. They stood around her, telling her what to write, with a kind of greed in their eyes. So much for discretion and anonymity.

'Everything all right, Ms Paige?' Rosamund

Harris, General Manager, was fighting her way through the throng. 'You know better than to bother the guests, Philip. I want to see you.'

'I didn't mean—'

'Now. My office. Sorry about that,' she cooed as the crowd dispersed. 'We do have strict rules. I do hope you weren't embarrassed.'

'Not at all,' Blair smiled. 'I'm used to it. Now, if you'll excuse us . . .'

'Of course, of course . . .'

As Rosamund Harris ushered them towards the entrance the young man remained in the same place, gazing after them, twisting the brochure in his hands. Ms Harris took it from him as she swept past. The autograph went straight into the first waste-paper bin she found.

'See what I mean?' Blair said as they went out. 'It's always like that. Just takes one and they're all on you. It's like opening the floodgates. And you want me to strip off!'

'He's very attractive,' Louise said, as they were getting into the car.

'Who is?'

'Chris James. The trainer guy.'

'Is he?' Blair replied. 'I don't really notice.'

Chapter 9

While they were at the gym, Della was hard at work in Felicity's office, sorting through all the fan mail forwarded to Blair by her film company.

'They send all of it?' Della asked.

'All of it,' Felicity replied, knowing the sort of mail the detective meant. 'I learnt in the States the importance of keeping inappropriate correspondence.' She unlocked a drawer and pulled out a bulky file. 'I store that kind separately.'

After her shower, Louise came to see what Della was doing.

'I see you survived,' the detective said, without looking up. 'How was it?'

'Fine. What are you doing?'

'Sorting through this lot.'

The letters were laid out on the desk in neat piles. They were written on every kind of paper from plain white, tissue thin, to deckle-edged pastel; but cheap ruled, torn from a spiral-bound pad or an exercise book, predominated.

Louise picked up a couple of pages. This was not your average fan mail. A quick glance confirmed that. She dropped one sheet and picked up another. The beginnings were all similar; formal, polite even, 'Dear Miss Paige', 'Dear Blair', but then, Louise's eyes widened as she read down one page and then another, 'I'd like to', 'I want to', 'I want you to' – they went on to describe exactly what they wanted to do, or wanted Blair to do to them; the language was mostly four-lettered, the detail pornographic. Louise let the pages drift back down to the table. It did not take long to overdose on that kind of hard-core fantasy. What kind of mind did it take to churn out that sort of garbage?'

'Does Blair read these?'

'Of course not. Felicity doesn't show them to her.'

'Why does she keep them?'

'Because they might be useful – as evidence. Careful with that one! Lift it by the corners.'

Della's voice rang out sharp. Louise looked at the card she'd just picked up. A valentine. What was special about that? There was nothing remarkable about the design or the sentiments expressed. Thousands were sold every year over the counters of newsagents, stationers, card shops everywhere in the country. The front showed a spray of flowers, a pink embossed heart. The message inside said 'I Love You'. Nothing remotely sinister. Except that it was five months too late.

'What's this doing with them?'

'We don't know exactly. It's no threat in itself,' Della added in answer to Louise's puzzled look, 'but it's odd. It rings a bell,' she frowned, 'but where, and why?' She shook her head. 'Another one came today. On the right. Typewritten address label. That's it. Take these if you want to open it.'

Louise used tweezers to ease the card from its envelope. The second valentine was black. The central heart-shaped cut-out was backed by crinkly red tissue. Except the colour was more rust than red, streaky and uneven. The white inset read 'LOVE ME', the sprawling letters in the same decayed shade.

'It looks like . . .' Louise began to say. She put the card down carefully, as if it could contaminate her.

'Blood. Yes it does. It'll probably be calf's blood or something,' Della added, to reassure herself as much as Louise. 'The only way to be certain is to have it analysed. There's a forensic scientist I know. I intend to drop it off at his lab. I'm going to see Leonora Quinn now. Do you want to come?'

'Yes. Sure.' Louise had never met an astrologer before.

Leonora Quinn was not how Louise had imagined her. She'd been vaguely expecting flowing robes and a crystal ball, but found instead an office full of computer terminals and fax machines.

The woman behind the wide corporate desk was wearing the expensive, understated, smartly elegant clothes of the female executive. She stood to welcome them.

'Ms Rivers, I presume.' The hand she extended was as small as a marmoset's. 'And you are?' She turned to Louise, her voice was melodious and surprisingly deep for someone so tiny.

'Louise Morgan. A friend of Blair's.'

Leonora nodded as though the girl merely confirmed what she knew already. Eyes, black and deeply set, swept over Louise and then returned to her face, darting this way and that like a scanner.

'Please be seated. Coffee?'

Louise was relieved when the woman turned back to Della.

An assistant entered the room with a tray.

'Help yourself to milk and sugar.'

'You wish to speak to me about my visit to Blair?' Leonora said as she handed them shallow cups of thin bone china.

'Yes. Do you mind if I tape this?'

Leonora shook her head. Della placed a Dictaphone on the desk, fiddling with the controls, glad of something to do. Even she felt unsettled by the older woman's penetrating scrutiny.

'What happened first?'

'I read the Tarot cards at Blair's request. I don't often use them but she insisted. I saw you there. The Queen of Swords,' she added, in reply to Della's questioning look. A tiny smile revealed small white teeth. 'A woman of formidable power and intellect who will offer her services to help and protect but will expect something in return for her efforts. I saw you, too.' She turned to Louise. 'The Knave of Cups – reflective and thoughtful, given to quiet contemplation, but generous and resourceful and gifted with great foresight.'

'Can I see the cards you use?' Louise asked, curious.

'Of course.'

The clairvoyant reached to a carved wooden box on the left side of the table, flipping it open as if she was about to offer them each a cigar. Inside the velvet lining was an oblong block wrapped in black silk. She spread the cards across the table. They were clearly very old. The card was worn to the texture of soft cloth by innumerable handlings. The exotic and arcane designs were finely engraved and richly coloured. You did not need to know what they symbolized to feel their power and fascination.

'Don't touch!' Leonora said sharply.

Louise snatched back her hand as if she'd been stung.

'Only the person who owns the cards is allowed to handle them,' Della explained.

'So,' Leonora raised the fine line of an immaculately plucked eyebrow, 'you're not a complete sceptic.'

'I have a friend who's interested, that's all.' She glanced back at the cards. They were a bit different from Janine's starter pack. 'So. How did it go?'

'Not well.' She moved the cards around recreating the spread, frowning at the images. 'You two were the only bright spots. Counter-indications at every stage. The same cards again and again. This is Blair.' She extracted the Queen of Cups. 'She was surrounded by these.' She picked out others and held them up, one after another. 'The Empress reversed, I take that to be that ghastly mother of hers; the Broken Tower, also reversed, an unlooked-for sudden event, a disaster.'

Leonora collected, and dealt again with crisp speed and a gambler's skill.

'King of Swords. Calculating, impersonal, deliberately sadistic. Knight of Swords. Headstrong, careless. All the cards reversed except your own.'

'Reversed? What does that mean?' Louise asked.

'The cards have a right and a wrong way up. If you receive it like this, it means one thing. Like that, quite another.'

'What happens if someone gets a bad spread like Blair did?' Louise asked. 'What do you say?'

'I terminate the reading. Say the cards are not working. But,' she paused, 'that wasn't all. It wasn't over.'

'You mean the flowers in the hall?' Della said.

Leonora nodded. 'Before I tell you about that, I'd like to explain something. These cards haven't been in my family for generations, handed down from mother to daughter, as my clients assume. I acquired them at auction. They cost a fortune. I bought them to impress. My kind of clientele expect the best.'

'So?' Della said, not sure where this was leading.

'I use them because they are good PR. I don't have the "sight", not like my mother, or my grandmother. My gran was a traveller, did the fairs from one end of the country to the other. She died in a layby on the A45, in a decrepit old trailer. My mother worked out of a caravan on the front at Brighton, telling fortunes to giggling girls for greasy fivers. I wanted more than that and my gift lay in a different direction. I took a degree in Business Studies.' She indicated the fax machines and computer terminals. 'I have databases on all my clients, links with news agencies, stock exchanges, the dealing floors in New York, Chicago, Tokyo, Hong Kong, Singapore. My predictions are based on accurate, detailed information from all over the world, constantly updated.'

'I still don't see . . .' Della frowned, still puzzled.

'I filter the knowledge I acquire through intuition and insight, detective work if you like – our callings are similar. I don't rely on psychic gifts any more than you do. The sight has been dormant in me for years, so I was as surprised as anyone, as you would be, by what happened.' She paused for a moment. 'I could sense it – right from the stairs – something evil.'

Roses. As clear as if they were in the room

here. A dozen at least, long stemmed, each one perfect, the blooms just about to unfurl; she could even smell their faint perfume. But as she approached, when she came close, they seemed to change, the heads bending until each one was drooping down covered in some kind of furry grey fungal decay.

'I could see both things at the same time, like one image on top of another, and the smell . . .' She passed a hand across her mouth as though wiping away the memory of vomit. 'The smell was disgusting, overpowering . . .'

Leonora's strong musical voice tailed off as a shuddering revulsion passed through her.

'And?' Della prompted her to go on.

'It's hard to explain, but I felt the touch, the merest brush, of a hand capable of the most terrible cruelty. And, unless I am very much mistaken, you have something in your possession from the same tainted source.'

Della's hand went down to her briefcase beside the chair. The second valentine was in there. Leonora's eyes on hers were black and bright, reflecting tiny pinpoints of light.

'The Queen of Swords reversed,' she said, 'can be too devious for her own good, beguiled by her own cleverness into only seeing half the truth. You be careful.'

Chapter 10

'Heather Griffiths!' Della exclaimed. 'The name I was trying to remember. You know, the valentine card? It's been bugging me since this morning. Do you mind if I drop you here?'

Della stopped outside the gates of Portland House and Louise got out. Della drove off thinking about Heather Griffiths. A local girl who had disappeared about four years ago. Della couldn't remember the exact details, but it had something to do with Valentine's Day. Maybe she'd disappeared then, or near then? No. It was to do with being sent stuff. Della gripped the steering wheel harder. It had to do with that. She added *Check Heather G,* to her mental list of things to do: *Card to Lab; Florist's.* She had been debating whether to follow up the flowers at all. The whole Leonora thing was tough to take, but Blair believed in her, and Blair was the client.

A Golf GTi broke through the afternoon heat shimmer. The driver was young, dark haired. He indicated and slowed to turn into Portland House. Stephen Franklin, Blair's brother. No one checked his entrance. Another 'authorized visitor'. She had met him briefly and then Felicity had told her some interesting things about him and his fractured family history.

Della adjusted her Ray Bans, her fingers tapping out a tune from the in-car stereo. She slowed, looking right, before turning off for Ashbury Village. Blair's brother or not, there was something not quite right about his particular story.

Della did not get back to Portland House until late afternoon. She slowed the car at the opened gates, but the guard waved her on; Della was now on the authorized visitor A-list. Halfway down the drive, she slowed again. Blair jogging with a guy. It must be Chris James. Della waited for them at the end of the drive. She wanted to meet him.

She accompanied them around to the back of the house. They were going for a swim. Blair invited Della to join them, but the detective had to decline, too busy.

'You could borrow one of Felicity's costumes – you must be about the same size. Go on, Della. It's such a hot day.' Blair wiped her face with the yellow bandanna she wore round her neck. 'I always forget how the weather can change . . .'

At the corner of the house, they met the guard Della had seen on early-morning patrol. One of the dogs barked and lunged forward. His handler pulled him back sharply.

'Sorry, Miss Paige.' The guard touched his cap in apology. 'It's just there's people here he don't recognize. If he can sniff clothes, or a hand. Hey!' His serious young face suddenly broke into a wide, wide smile. 'Chris! How you doin', man?'

'Fine, Roy. How about you?'

They feigned a few jabs and then clasped hands.

'What are you doing here?'

Chris laughed. 'Working – same as you.'

'Ain't seen you down the gym for a while . . .'

Chris shrugged. 'Been busy. I try to be there Fridays . . .'

'That right? Maybe I'll come down then. It's good to see you, man!' He leaned down to his dogs. 'See this guy – he's a friend. Take a good long sniff. That's it.' The dog growled at Della. The young guard grinned. 'Her, too.'

Louise was out on the wooden deck, her lounger next to Stephen's. Behind them, the sliding glass wall of the indoor pool was open. They seemed to be getting on very well, lying, heads together, laughing, when the others arrived.

'Hi, Steve,' Chris said, as he went past and into the pool. 'I didn't know you were here.'

'Hi,' Stephen muttered and lay back, eyes closed, in sullen silence.

'Are you coming in?' his sister asked.

'No,' Stephen answered without even opening his eyes.

'What's the matter with him?' Blair mouthed.

Louise shrugged, *search me*. They had been in and out of the pool all afternoon, swimming, fooling around. Stephen was a good laugh, easy to be with, and an excellent swimmer, with the strong powerful stroke and tireless stamina of a water polo player. Now, quite suddenly, he didn't want to know.

Della raised an eyebrow. It was quite clear to her what was wrong here. Dislike crackled between the two men like static electricity. Perhaps she'd take up Blair's offer of a swim after all.

Della went in but Louise stayed with Stephen.

'I didn't know you knew Chris,' she said.

'Met him in LA when Blair was making that diving film.' Stephen stood up. 'I'm going in now, you coming?'

Louise looked at him from behind her sunglasses. Maybe he felt physically inferior, she thought, some guys got sensitive about comparisons. Just as quickly, she dismissed the possibility. He might not have Chris's latex-coated corrugated steel physique but there was nothing wrong with Stephen's wide-shouldered, narrow-hipped, swimmer's build. He was smooth skinned and flat muscled, slim, but not puny.

'Well? Are you staying, or what?'

'No. I'll come with you.'

As they walked back in the early evening cool, the silence between them lengthened like the shadows across the lawn. It occurred to Louise that he was showing all the signs and symptoms of being jealous.

Della came out in her borrowed costume and stood on the edge of the water. It was a nice pool.

Wide curving steps led into the shallow end and fifteen metres away a classical statue stared down at a mosaic of dolphins, grey and white, through the blue of the deeper water. There was a spring-board at the far end, but it was pushed up against the wall, not in use. Della wondered if Blair ever practised diving, now the film was over.

Blair was already swimming up and down. Chris James was walking the side of the pool scolding and encouraging, criticizing and correcting what seemed to be an already immaculate swimming style. Della walked down the steps and pushed off into the deeper water, hoping he wasn't going to look at hers too closely.

Blair pulled herself out; Della was still swimming her long strong crawl. Chris James dived in, taking over the laps, arrowing up and down with the smooth practised stroke and tumble turns of a competition swimmer. Della waited at one end, sitting on the side as he completed his length.

'Hi, Chris. Can I have a word?'

He turned as if to swim again. She had to lean out and tap him on the back to get his attention.

'Sorry. Didn't hear. I have to wear these,' he said, taking little plastic plugs out of both ears.

'You swim well. Ever been in competition?'

'A bit.' He laughed and boosted himself out to sit on the side, legs dangling in the water. 'You're not so bad yourself.'

'Where did you train?'

'Jubilee Baths. Off the Western Road. Do you know it?'

Della laughed. 'Used to go there when I was a kid. That's where I learnt.'

He grinned. 'Small world.'

It certainly is. Della hadn't thought of the place for years in any conscious way, but fragments of memory came back to her. Looking down from the wrought-iron balcony, the diving boards descending like giant steps, white chequered tiles, creating weird optical effects, until she felt she was about to fall into the glassy surface of the water. As a young child, she had been fascinated by the cubicles they provided for people without bathrooms. Once a dead tramp had been found in one of the stained enamel baths. He had probably dossed there, but in Della's imagination he was up to his neck in water.

'They're knocking it down.'

'Sorry?' It took a moment for Della to recollect herself.

'The old pool. It's all moved up to the new Leisure Centre.'

'I haven't been there – any good?'

'Olympic-length pool, wave machine, flumes, the whole bit. No platforms, though.'

'Platforms?'

'For diving. Diving was my sport, till I did my ears in.'

'Oh, right. Of course. I was too scared to even jump off, let alone dive.' Della laughed again. 'Used to crawl to the edge and then chicken out.

It's a shame they closed it. At least it was a proper pool for swimming. I can't relax if I think a dozen screaming kids are about to land on top of me.'

He laughed. 'I know what you mean. There was no messing around at the other place – not when my dad ran it.'

'Your dad was the manager?'

'Sort of. And coach. You did a bit of everything in those days. Kids at school called me Chlorine.'

'Hey – maybe your dad coached my brother.'

'Might have. He a swimmer?'

'Not now. He was. Dead keen for a while but swimming training is a punishing routine for a kid. Don't you think?'

Chris James shrugged. 'You get used to it.'

'Too tough for Mark. He gave it up for football.'

'Mark Rivers?' he said, shaking his head. 'I don't . . .'

'No reason why you should, he's younger than you. Twenty-two now. So he'd have been maybe thirteen, fourteen . . .'

'Sorry, don't remember him. Now, if you don't mind, I'll hit the shower . . .'

'Sure. Me too.' She stood up with him. 'One more thing. Did you know a girl called Heather Griffiths?'

'Why do you ask?' The name sparked something in his deep dark eyes but he kept his bland expression, touching a hand to the sides of his smiling mouth smoothing down the skin.

'Just thought you might. She was a swimmer.'

'The kid who disappeared? Yes, I remember

her. She was one of my dad's protégées. I didn't coach her, or know her all that well.' He shook his head. 'Terrible thing at the time.'

'Did the police question you?' Della asked.

'No. As I said, I hardly knew her. How long ago was it?'

'About four years.'

'And they never found her?'

'No.' Della shook her head. 'They never did. I guess you know why I'm here – so if you see anyone acting suspicious . . .'

'Of course. There's one thing I can personally guarantee.' He folded his arms. Solid biceps bulged against flesh. 'Blair's safe enough with me. If I see anything, anyone, you'll be the first to know. Nice meeting you, Della.'

The detective watched him go. Time to give Mark a call. He was still her little brother, after all. She would ring him as soon as she got back. He'd probably be out, but she could leave a message.

Chapter 11

There was a gentle knock on Louise's door.

'Hi. It's me.'

It was Stephen. A shower and a change of clothes seemed to have sweetened his mood. He came in, ready to apologize.

'Too much sun. Must have been out there too long,' he said with a smile, teeth white against the beginnings of a tan. 'I was wondering if you'd let me make it up to you?'

'There's really no need . . .' Louise started to say.

'Even if there isn't,' his smile widened, 'I'd still like to take you out.'

'What? Now?'

'Yes. I thought we could find somewhere to eat – there's a new pizza place, Felicity says it's supposed to be good. And then, it's such a nice evening, I thought maybe we could drive out, find a pub somewhere. What do you say?'

The pizza place, all art deco chrome and steel, had only just opened. It was spacious inside, but popular; they had to wait a while. Sitting at the bar, Stephen apologized again for his poolside behaviour.

'It's that Chris James.' Stephen fiddled with his

glass, turning it round on the paper coaster. 'I can't stand the guy.'

'Why? What's wrong with him?' Louise was genuinely surprised. She thought Chris was nice.

'He's so, I don't know, proprietorial about Blair, it's like he owns her. All that training they do together. It's unnecessary. She's not an Olympic athlete, or anything.'

'She could have been,' Louise remarked.

'How do you know?'

'Chris told me, this morning at the health club.'

Stephen grimaced. 'Don't tell me you've fallen under his spell as well?' He shook his head. 'That level of training is not necessary. It could even be damaging.' He laughed cynically. 'Unless they're using it as an excuse, of course.'

'For what?'

He laughed again. 'Come on, Louise. Don't be naive. What do you think?'

They were shown to a table then, and their talk turned to other things. Stephen told her about his life as a medical student, his ambitions to become a doctor. He'd already decided he wanted to be an orthopaedic surgeon, specializing in sporting injuries. He made his mind up after he had spent some time up at the university hospital in the sports injury clinic. That's where he met Penny, his ex-girlfriend. She had been referred by her GP with a cartilage problem in her right knee.

'It's very common in people who do a lot of aerobics, keep-fit, dance-based exercise. Running too – that's why I worry about Blair. I've seen enough cases. What happens is – imagine this is the knee.' He took a piece of bread and bent it at 45 degrees. 'Each movement puts strain here and here,' he worked the bread backwards and forwards, 'on the cartilage. Eventually it can snap, or bits fall off and get under the kneecap. If it gets really bad we suck out all the little gravelly bits and replace the damaged cartilage.' He dipped the bread into a small bowl of garlic and olive oil and bit into it. 'The procedure can be painful,' he chewed thoughtfully, 'but it's usually pretty successful. Are you all right?' he asked. Louise had gone quite pale. 'Don't you want that?'

'No, it's OK.' Louise pushed away the rest of her *quattro stagioni*. 'You can finish it.'

On their way out he plucked a carnation from the tall vase at the centre of the table and presented it to her by way of apology for his gruesome dinner conversation.

'I'm sorry. I get so used to talking about bodies and bits over canteen beans and chips, I forget not everyone is used to it. No more medical stuff, I promise.'

He was as good as his word. The pub he took her to had a garden. They sat there until closing time, talking about everything except medicine. The night was warm and the scent from the roses and old-fashioned cottage flowers made it far more pleasant outside than in the crowded bar with its pool table and clouds of cigarette smoke.

'I used to go to school not far from here. When we were in the sixth form we used to sneak out for a game and a beer.'

'You were at boarding school?'

'I was sent there when my parents split up. I thought Gina would take the both of us, me and Blair, to live with her. I know it sounds stupid now, but I saw myself taking Dad's place, you know, the man of the family? Fat chance.' His face twisted into a cynical grin. 'I was packed off as soon as Gina could find a place which would take me.'

'Why didn't you stay with your dad?'

'He didn't want me, either.' Stephen's answer was completely matter-of-fact, as if he was discussing the weather.

'That's awful!' Louise was genuinely shocked.

'There was no choice. But it got better. By the time I started coming here it was almost tolerable.' He took a drink. 'You know, all the time I was at school I never told anyone I was Blair's brother.'

Louise could understand that. She rarely talked about her to anyone either.

'Didn't they ask about your family?'

'Not much. If anyone did I just told them I had a sister who lived in the States. My mother went there when my folks broke up. They could relate to that. Lots of them had divorced parents, brothers and sisters all over the place. I just didn't say who my sister was.' He put down his glass.

'It sounds like I'm boasting, or cashing in, or living off reflected glory.'

'Yeah,' Louise agreed. 'If you mention it people go out of their way to say something spiteful.'

'Or worse. You know what boys are like. Given the sort of films she's been in it was better to keep quiet about it. I didn't even tell Penny at first.'

'Why not?'

'She's kind of the jealous type—'

'But Blair's your sister!'

'I know. It's not so much her – it's the fame/success bit. Penny can't handle it. She thinks, "Why not me?" You know?'

Louise nodded. There were people who saw success in others as a threat, a slight to themselves. Maybe Penny was like that.

'I had to tell her eventually, of course.'

'How did she react?'

'Difficult to tell. Mad at me for not telling her, then she kind of went into herself. We didn't talk about it. But Pen does tend to bottle things up. Finds it hard to discuss her feelings. I'm empty. Would you like another?'

'Yes, OK.'

He went off to the bar and Louise sat back in her chair, enjoying the soft night air. Stephen was certainly attractive and very good company, but she had to be careful. There was something about him, a kind of distance, and when he talked about Penny, it was always in the present tense.

'Are you desperate to get back?' Stephen asked. The man had called 'Last orders, please', and they were ready to leave.

'No. But where can we go this time of night?'

'Lots of places. I was thinking about one in particular.'

'Oh? Where?'

'Warnock.'

'But that's miles!'

The Warnock was the local name for a famous beauty spot, a ridge of ancient hills marking the western edge of the flat midland plain. The craggy sandstone cliffs reared above the flat landscape and the views were dramatic, but it was now night time and the Warnock Hills were a long way from here.

'So? It's such a nice night, seems a shame to waste it.'

'People go there for the view. What is there to see in the dark?'

'You'd be surprised.'

He pulled off the road and on to a country track going up into the hills. The moon shone through the trees, toning daytime colours to blue and grey.

'Dad used to bring us when we were kids. There's a big space at the top where we flew kites. We used to play hide and seek in the trees. Blair was good at hiding and it would take me ages to find her. I remember once getting really worried; I thought I'd lost her, and then there she was, curled up fast asleep. She looked so perfect; it was like finding Snow White or a kid out of a fairy tale.' He stopped the car and sat, arms folded, as the engine ticked and cooled. 'Later, when I was at school, I used to come out here on the bus.'

'On your own?'

'Yes.' He looked over at her and laughed. 'That was the point. You haven't been to a boarding school, have you?'

'No.'

'Imagine being with your class twenty-four hours a day, every day, no breaks, no privacy. I came here to get away from them.' He frowned and stared down, his eyes shuttered, his voice quiet. 'I really hated it there, particularly at the beginning. Gina was so keen to get rid of me, she didn't even wait around for the start of a term. It was awful. I didn't know anybody. I didn't know all the stupid names and little rituals. They'd all been together since the beginning of the year, so I was fresh meat.'

'How old were you?'

'Fourteen. Going on fifteen. But I was kind of small and puny, hormones hadn't kicked in. I took some real stick. Cruelty you wouldn't believe, from having the crap beaten out of you, to refined mental torture. All I wanted to do was run away, but where to? Can you imagine being homesick when there's no home to go to?'

'How do you feel about her now? Gina, I mean?'

'I survived, didn't I?' Stephen shrugged, arms folded. 'Water under the bridge.'

They sat in silence. Stephen gazed straight ahead out at the silvery tree trunks in front of him, the expression unreadable on his deeply shadowed face.

'Come on,' he said eventually.

'Where are we going?'

'You'll see.'

He took her hand and led her through the trees. Oaks and beeches gave way to pine, needles crackled underfoot and the air still held the resinous scent released by the day's heat. At the top was a sandy clearing dotted with outcropping rock.

'Did you know,' he put his arm round her, 'that the human eye can pick out the light of a candle at ten miles' distance?'

Fields, hills and woods spread out below them in different grades of shadow. Single farms, hamlets and villages winked like fireflies. The motorway showed like a necklace of light strung across the blackness and far to the east lay the suffused neon of the city.

'I like places like this,' he said, his voice near. 'Wild places, lonely places. Even down there,' he pointed towards the orange glow which marked the vast conurbation, 'you can find them if you know where to look. There's one near where I live, right next to the university, hemmed in on all sides, a stretch of pure country. I go there sometimes to get away from people. Well, Penny, mostly. You know what it's like when you really care about someone, but you just can't seem to get through . . .' He turned so his face was very close to hers. 'Or maybe you don't.' His voice was soft now, less bitter. 'Maybe you're too young to know about things like that.'

'I know,' Louise said quietly. 'That's how it got with Matt and me. Except it was him who packed it in eventually.'

'Did he? He must have been crazy.'

Long lashes, dark as charcoal, brushed down and his face blurred as it came towards her. Stubble grazed her chin and cheek but his mouth on hers was warm and soft.

'We'd better be getting back,' he said after what seemed like a long time. 'You're cold, you're shivering. I shouldn't have – I'm sorry.'

'For what?' Louise asked, wrapping her arms about herself. She was shivering, but not from the cold.

'Bringing you here, keeping you out. I don't know what came over me.' He draped his coat round her shoulders. 'I shouldn't have . . . It's just that I find you very attractive . . .'

Louise broke away. Confronted by Blair's perfection and faultless beauty, her own physical attractiveness had been much in her mind lately. Besides, it sounded like a fake chat-up line. Why did he have to spoil it when they'd been getting on so well?

'What's the matter? Where are you going?' He caught up with her and turned her round. 'I meant what I said . . .'

'Really?'

'Yes! Or I wouldn't have said it!'

'It's just . . .' Louise looked away. 'I don't think that. Not compared to Blair.' She hadn't meant to say it, but the words were out. 'She has that effect,' she added, unable to explain, needing to cover herself. 'Not intentionally, but she does.'

'You shouldn't compare. It's not fair on either of you.'

He took her arm and they walked back to the car in silence.

He started the engine. 'We'd better get you home, hadn't we?'

'I'm not a child, you know,' Louise snapped.

He turned to her, surprised by her annoyance, and then he cut the ignition.

'No,' he murmured as he released his seatbelt and reached across the space between them. 'I don't suppose you are.'

Chapter 12

Blair lay on the couch in the vast living room, remote in hand, switching TV channels. The day was bright and promised heat, but she did not feel like going out. She felt lethargic, but tense at the same time. Chris had phoned to cancel their early-morning run; he was busy. That annoyed her. Della was with Felicity, being big girls together. That annoyed her. If they were keeping things back from her, Blair would like to know exactly who was paying them. She stretched; the tension in her shoulders was reaching screaming pitch.

'You ought to try and relax more.'

Blair laughed as Louise came in. 'Tell me about it. Where did you go with Stephen?'

'We went for a pizza and then he took me out to a pub in the country.'

'Until two in the morning?'

'We went for a drive.'

Blair's eyebrows rose. 'I see.'

Louise could feel herself blushing. 'We were talking.'

'Oh, what about?'

'You mostly. Where is he? Have you seen him this morning?'

'I think he's gone for a walk, or something.'

Louise looked at the garden and grounds,

vaguely sorry that he had not waited, invited her to go with him.

'Do you want to go out?' She turned to Blair. 'Maybe we'll meet him. This is so beautiful. It's a shame not to enjoy it.'

Blair stood up. 'I've got a better idea. Let's go have a swim and sauna. We can go for a walk after.'

Della had come to check the mail.

'Has anything else arrived?'

'Doesn't seem to have.' Felicity looked up from the pile of correspondence she had just opened. 'Nothing. Two days running. Perhaps that's the end of it.' She smiled and invited Della to join her in a cup of coffee.

'I wouldn't count on it,' the detective said, declining the offer. 'I'll be out of the office until this afternoon. If you want to reach me I'll be on the mobile.'

'Quick swim and then into the sauna,' Blair said, as they both jumped into the still blue water.

A pine door at the back of the swimming pool led into the sauna. They hung up their dripping costumes and stepped into the hot pine-scented air. The cabin was big enough for six to eight. Blair and Louise stretched out on opposite benches.

'That's better. Much better.' Blair lay on her

front. Her body was a uniform golden brown, no bikini- or strap-marks, no blemishes marred the smooth tanned surface of her skin.

Louise covered herself with a towel. She had caught the sun yesterday and now looked like she was wearing a white bathing suit. The heat was building. Blair was soaking it up, but Louise, not used to saunas, was finding it unbearable.

'Can we have the door open?' she asked.

'That destroys the whole point!' Blair laughed. 'All right, just a crack.'

She stood, to push the heavy pine door, shoulder muscles moving under her silky skin, sliding across her back.

'Tell you what.' She was standing by the coals now with a jug in her hand. 'I'll put this on.'

'What is it?'

'Water with essential oils that Margery at the health club gave me. She's the masseuse. It's her own special secret recipe.'

Blair threw the scented water on to the coals. The desert-dry air was suddenly transformed to tropical wetness. Louise felt the sweat break out all over her.

Blair leaned back on the bench opposite, laughing at Louise's reaction. Blair was not skinny, or even all that thin, Louise realized, but there was not an ounce of fat on her. Long legs, flat stomach, skin taut over rippled muscles.

'What are you staring at?' Blair asked, laughter fading.

'You,' Louise said simply. 'How do you get to be that perfect?'

'Hard work.' Blair stretched out on her back. 'I work at it. I see it as my job, a responsibility to myself. Like you study for exams, I work out so I can perform well in the parts I play. That's why Chris is so important to me.'

'About Chris . . .'

'What about him?'

'Have you two got a thing going?'

'Why do you ask?' Blair's tone was sharper now, less relaxed. 'Has Stephen been talking to you?'

'No. Well, yes . . .'

'I thought he might. He was so rude to Chris yesterday. It was the same in LA. What's it got to do with him? He needs to learn not to treat me like a child and to mind his own business.'

There was silence between them. Louise was uncomfortably aware that the last remark probably applied to her as well.

'The answer to your question is no,' Blair said, as she turned over. 'There is nothing between us. Gina would go ape and the tabloids would have a field day. You have to understand, Louise,' she added, 'I have my reputation, I'm not about to jeopardize it by going with the hired help.'

It was not any kind of noise, it was more a change in the air, an almost imperceptible displacement, that could have told them that there was someone else in the sauna. But both girls were deeply asleep, relaxed by the heat, drugged by the exotic oils' heady perfume.

He stood for a moment looking down. Blair's back was exposed to him, her thick black hair parted, tumbling over her shoulders almost to the floor. He looked at the soft nape of her neck, at the long muscles stretching down either side of the spine. His hand trembled. The razor shimmered, bright like a fish in sunlight. It flashed as he brought it down in one swift sure movement and a length of Blair's hair fell like smoke descending. He bent to gather the lock before it reached the floor, and then he withdrew, closing the door to the exact crack of space that Blair had left.

Louise woke quickly, perhaps warned by some deep sixth sense. She sat up, looking round, but nothing seemed to have changed, everything seemed the same.

'I feel much better.' Blair opened her eyes and smiled. 'See? I told you it was relaxing. Now we go for a swim.'

'What?' Louise looked down at herself. 'Like this?'

Blair opened the door of the sauna.

'Of course like this. Why do you think people have private pools?'

'What if someone sees?'

Blair laughed. 'Like who?'

'I don't know.' Louise joined her friend at the door. 'Like Roy, he might be patrolling . . .'

'And he might not. I know what the matter is. You're scared to go in.'

Blair seized Louise, pinning her arms, pushing her to the edge of the pool.

'No, Blair. Please! No!'

But it was too late. Louise was already underwater. The pool was kept at almost blood heat, but it felt glacial on Louise's super-heated skin. She surfaced, spluttering, but it was kind of exhilarating once you got used to it.

Blair jumped in beside her. Louise swam over, pushing her under. Soon they were playing, chasing and splashing, shrieking and laughing like they were kids again in the public pool.

Louise was sculling on her back in the deep end under the shadow of the diving board. Blair was sitting on the side.

'Blair?' Louise called over. 'Will you do something for me? Will you dive for me?'

'OK.' Blair shook out her hair and went over to the board. 'Get out of the way, then. I don't want to land on top of you.'

Blair mounted the springboard. Its up-down movement synchronized to her stepping. She drove with one leg and the board leapt. She hit the end with both feet, perfectly balanced. The flexing motion powered her high into the air. She seemed to fly above the water, arms out and back from the shoulders, then her body pivoted, arms extended above her head for a perfect entry.

She can do it. She can really do it! Louise stared amazed.

'Do it again!' she called, and Blair obliged.

Blair chose a forward layout with a half twist for her second dive. Louise did not know, but this was one of the most delicate and difficult of dives; it was so easy for the body to get out of line and out of balance. She synchronized her steps, using the momentum of the board, driving down into the hurdle, landing perfectly to soar up into the air. All the time she could hear Chris's voice, talking her through it.

'Head up, arms slightly in front, above the shoulders, point your arm at the water to rotate. Keep on the same plane, look front, not too much, you'll flatten the dive, too far behind you'll push over. Through the crest, sight the water, moving round, back to the water now, use your head and arms, align yourself. Stretch with your feet, drive with your chest, close your arms. Enter.'

Louise did not know any of the technicalities. She just saw Blair turning high in the air, arms outstretched, arcing round, her back to the board now, to enter the water with barely a whisper.

'That was fantastic!' she said when Blair swam to the side. 'Will you teach me?'

'Hey,' Blair shook the hair out of her eyes, 'it's not as easy as it looks, you know, and I'm no coach.'

'Oh go on . . .'

'OK.' Blair boosted herself out. 'Come on, then.'

Girls laughing, the sound thinned by distance, still carried. He sat in the tree he had chosen, deep in the woods, adjusting the focus of the binoculars. Somewhere a dog barked. Time to go. Such a shame. Just when he was having a good time. He had so enjoyed the exhibition diving – faultless technique – and the two of them frolicking like a pair of water nymphs had hardly been less entertaining. Still, it paid to be careful and he had already loitered here longer than intended. His mission here was accomplished and he had other business. He dropped to the ground. In his pocket he carried two precious mementos of his visit.

Chapter 13

The phone rang as Janine was leaving the office.

'I'm afraid she's not here right now, Ms Chambers,' Janine said. 'She's due back this afternoon. Can I help?'

'No.' The reply came crisp and quick from Blair Paige's PA. 'I need to speak to her personally.'

'Have you tried her mobile? I can give you the number . . . Already tried that, right. OK. I'll leave a note on her desk.'

Janine wrote a note for Della before going downstairs to collect Mandy. They had lunch together every day in a little veggie place round the corner. Della thought it was dippy and New Age, but Janine and Mandy enjoyed the ambience.

The copy of the *Post* Janine held under her arm carried Leonora Quinn's astrology column. Mandy was Libra, Janine Gemini; that's why they got on so well. Studying their stars was a lunch-time ritual and Leonora Quinn was their favourite. Her forecasts were by far the most accurate. Janine couldn't wait to tell Mandy that Della had actually been to see Leonora.

The phone chirrupped inside Della's car, unheard. The detective was twenty yards away, sitting on a wall in one of the city's more desirable residential districts, about half a mile from the university. She was working on gaining entry to the large detached house opposite. Three-storey late Victorian Gothic, fronting the road on two sides, steps leading between double bays to a roofed porch. Once it must have belonged to a prosperous family, but it was now divided into flats.

She stepped between the cars parked outside. Seven buzzers on the side of the porch. Number 7: Penny Harbury. Her label contained space for another name. Stephen Franklin had been erased. Della tried the buzzer again.

The top half of the front door was glass. Through the opaque ribbed glass in the top half of the door, Della could see someone moving about. She tapped lightly and stepped back.

'Hi! Sorry to bother you – could you let me in? I just popped out to move the car – parked on double yellows . . .'

She gave a shrug and a you-know-how-it-is grin. The woman smiled, vaguely sympathetic, as she opened the door.

Della climbed the mahogany staircase. The flats were numbered from one; Penny's was right at the top. There was no bell so she rapped on the door, then knocked again, louder. She was beginning to think there really was no one home, when an eye peered out of the bulging spy hole. A chain rattled and the lock was drawn back by a tall girl in a crumpled T-shirt. She was undeniably pretty, but her blue eyes were dull, ringed with shadows. She looked as faded and washed out as her old black leggings.

'Do I know you?' She leaned on the door frame, sweeping long strings of greasy brown hair back from her face.

'Er, no. Not exactly. Hi,' Della started, smiling and friendly. She was dressed in student gear, jeans, sweatshirt, and trainers. 'I'm Jill Carey. Mature student, MA in Social Anthropology.' Her opening line was met by incomprehension, but the door remained open. Della went on, the next few seconds vital if she was to get inside. 'I heard you might want someone to share. I don't usually knock on people's doors, but I've been looking for that long . . .'

'Where did you hear that?'

'On the grapevine. A friend of a friend in your building.'

The girl shrugged and turned but left the door open.

'Come in.' She led the way into the flat. 'It's a bit of a mess, I just . . .' The girl shrugged, the rest of the sentence unexpressed. She sank onto the sofa and lit a cigarette.

The flat took up the whole top floor of the house. The living room was big, with sloping attic ceilings and a pretty Victorian fireplace. The furnishings were cheap but stylish, a confident combination of junk shop bargains and Ikea basics. The sun poured in a solid shaft through the partially opened curtains onto bright rugs scattered over polished floors. A pleasant room, but it smelt stale, ashtrays overflowed, the remains of a Chinese takeaway decayed inside aluminium boxes.

Della sat in a blue rattan chair, after first removing a ginger cat and a dirty towel. The cat yowled in protest and went to the girl, rubbing against her legs. She ignored him. Don and Jill chatted on lunchtime TV. She ignored them as well.

'He's not mine.' She pushed at the cat with her bare foot. 'He belongs to Stephen.' As she said his name, tiny cramps of pain creased her forehead. 'Boyfriend. Ex-boyfriend,' she corrected. 'Managed to leave his cat behind.'

She exhaled deeply and stubbed out her cigarette. There were tears behind the sigh.

'I'm sorry. I really must pull myself together.' She spoke quietly, as if to herself, before turning to Della. 'You are?' she shook her head, 'I've forgotten already . . .'

'Jill Carey.' Della leant over. The hand that took hers was thin and cold. 'MA student – Social Anthropology.'

'Penny Harbury. Education,' she smiled weakly. 'We sound like *University Challenge*.' She wiped her face with her fingers. 'I must apologize. I'm not always like this. To be honest, I hadn't even thought about getting anyone else in – he only moved out a week ago and I'm still a bit cut up.'

'Look. I called at a bad time – I'm sorry.' Della

put on an expression full of concern. 'It's just when I heard there was a chance of a place here, it's such a nice area and so close to the university, I jumped at it. They go so quick and I'm that desperate.' She frowned as though recalling worries of her own. 'But I'd better be going.' She reached down for her bag. 'I've obviously got the wrong end of the stick.'

'No. Don't go. It's a good idea – I could do with someone to share the rent; it's too much for me really. I had this notion he might come back – but there's not much chance of that. God, how stupid.' Her sigh was dry of tears this time, and suggested harsher emotions, jealousy, anger even, lying behind her surface despair. 'I've hardly been out, just sat here thinking, dreaming up ways . . . Do you want a cup of tea?' Penny said, suddenly recalling herself.

'Yes, if it's not too much trouble . . .'

'No trouble. You're the first person I've seen for days. I honestly think I might go crazy if I don't talk to someone. There isn't any milk, I drank all the coffee. Will herbal do?'

'Herbal's fine.'

Della got up while Penny was in the kitchen. The room doubled as a study. A desk over in the corner held a computer in amongst a litter of disks, papers and books. The drawer was wrenched wide open, spilling out a jumble of stationery.

Desks were interesting. Desks told you a lot about a person. Della drifted over, as if to admire the view from the window beside it, and sifted through the surface chaos. Didn't this girl ever use a bin? Della pushed aside an empty HMV bag to see what was underneath. Nothing of any great interest.

You could see the university tower from here. It dominated this part of the city. Della pulled the curtain back and looked out as her hand flicked with practised swiftness through the contents of the open drawer. Writing paper, envelopes, cards. Penny was the sort of person who bought cards in advance and kept them in reserve. Birthday, Get Well, Good Luck and, shoved away, underneath them all, valentines. The design looked similar. Della smuggled one out and put it in her pocket.

'I'm sorry to be so disorganized . . .' Penny was returning.

Della resumed her seat and accepted a mug of straw-coloured tea. It was time to make her move.

'If it's any consolation, I know how you feel . . .' she said quietly, confiding, sympathetic, gazing through the thin steam of the sharp-smelling brew, fine-tuning her expression to convince the girl she was a fellow emotional casualty.

'Do you?' Penny left her tea. Her fingers began to shred an empty red stamp book, her eyes on Della, greedy to share, to know if her pain had been suffered by another. 'Really?'

'Oh, yes I do.' Della gave her wan thin smile just the right twist of bitterness. 'Believe me.'

Round the corner, Della checked back with Janine for messages. The office was on answer-phone. She called Portland House.

'Hi, Louise? It's me.' Della's car idled in the queue at the traffic lights. 'Listen. Is Stephen around?'

'Not right here. I can go and find him, if you like.'

'No, don't do that. I've just been to see the girlfriend. They're not telling the same story. And there's other stuff . . .'

'What other stuff?'

'Stuff that doesn't add up. I ran a credit check. He's in debt, and the flowers were ordered on one of his cards . . .'

'Della. Listen. Felicity—'

'Got to go,' Della cut in. 'The lights are changing.'

'Della!' Louise found herself talking to the tone.

Mobiles sound different from ordinary phones, the sound seems to wax and wane in empty space, punctuated with stray noise and ticks. The hollow, echoey quality of the call could have been due to this, but the following click sounded near, like someone on another line had just put down the receiver.

Chapter 14

Della went from Penny's flat to a hospital lab on the other side of the city. Her pet forensic scientist, Dr Brian Western, had been analysing the valentine card; he was doing the work in his own time, so she had to wait for his report. The delay made her late and the cross-town traffic was murder. Roadworks and homeward-bound commuters. Della sat in the sweating queues, glowering at other motorists, consumed with anxiety.

Western's report was brief. It read:

SPECIES: HUMAN
TYPE: A Rh NEG
YOU OWE ME A PINT – BUT I'LL SETTLE FOR GUINNESS!

The last was Brian's idea of a joke, but Della was not in joking mood. Type A Rhesus Negative was not rare, but neither was it common. The sample itself was not that important. They couldn't match it without the donor. Soaking pieces of tissue paper in it, using it as ink, then sending that through the post, that was the important bit. Della wondered if Penny was capable of doing that. She seemed too flaky, but what if she was working with someone else?

Della pulled her shirt away from her back,

cursing the slow snail creep of the traffic, hitting her horn, yelling out of her window at a motorist who was trying to cut her up.

When she got to her building Janine and Mandy, the receptionist from downstairs, were gossiping in the stairwell.

'Who is he, anyway?'

'Market research. He was in my office the other day. He can research me any time he wants to.'

'I didn't really get a look . . .' Janine said, wishing she'd taken more interest.

'He fancies you.'

'How do you know?'

'He kept looking at you. He might be in the caff again.' Mandy giggled. 'D'you fancy a bit of carrot cake?'

'No she doesn't,' Della growled.

'Oh, hi, Della. There's a visitor upstairs been waiting for you.'

'I want you upstairs, too,' Della said as she went past. 'Not down here gossiping. And don't disappear to that café.'

'OK,' Janine shrugged, sulkily. 'I wasn't going to. It's too late, now, anyway. It'll be closing soon.'

'All right.' Della tried a smile. 'Sorry.'

'He might be there tomorrow,' Mandy giggled again. 'He's dead fit for an older guy, you'd be just right . . .'

'Do you mind?' Janine replied. 'I'm only twenty-five . . .'

Mandy laughed. 'You know what I mean . . .'

Mandy was seventeen. To her, everyone over twenty was ready to draw their pension.

'Yeah, well . . .'

Della mounted the stairs and closed the office door on the last wisps of conversation.

Felicity was waiting in Della's office. There was something she wished to discuss with the detective and she preferred to do so away from Portland House.

'Hello, Felicity. What's up? Has anything else come?'

The PA shook her head.

'What can I do for you, then?'

'I'm concerned about the level of protection Blair is getting. It's not a criticism of you, it's just – one of the guards, Roy, thought someone was in the woods.'

'Did he send the dogs in?'

'Yes, but they lost the scent, apparently.' She paused, as though weighing her next words. 'I think I'd be a whole lot happier if the police were involved at this stage.'

Della leaned back in her chair, considering, then she said, 'I don't disagree with you. But it's not my decision. It will be up to Blair to decide.'

'I will discuss it with her, and Gina, of course. But I wanted to talk to you first. I didn't want you to think I had no confidence in you.'

'I wouldn't think that. As long as you realize

the police aren't going to wave any magic wands. If Blair wants to bring them in I will offer my full cooperation.'

'There's another thing.' Felicity bit her lip. 'Gina's thinking of cutting short Blair's visit here.'

'Oh? Where's she thinking of going?'

'London, of course.'

Della gave a humourless laugh. 'What's the point of that? He'll just follow her. Why doesn't she take her right out of the country?'

'Blair's committed to another round of publicity over the next few weeks following her film's UK release.'

'If you want to move, I'd do so in a day or two. No panic decisions, find somewhere secure. Meanwhile guards and the police give two lines of defence. He might think twice about breaching that . . .'

'It makes Blair a prisoner in her own house.' Felicity stood up to leave. 'She won't like that.'

'She'll be a prisoner anywhere unless he's stopped.'

Della followed Felicity to the door. Increased security might deal with external threats, but what if the danger was not from without? What if it was coming from inside the house?

'I'm coming with you.' Della locked her office for the night. 'I want a word with Stephen.'

Chapter 15

Stephen was not at Portland House. He and Louise had gone out for the evening. They were supposed to be going for a drive, but they ended up going to the movies, at the multiplex, the one Louise had visited with Blair. He bought the tickets and they sat in the dark watching his sister. Louise divided her attention between the screen and watching him crushing his cola cup, tearing it to bits.

Stephen left before the end, barging along the row, leaving Louise to follow, muttering apologies for the disturbance they were causing.

'What was that about?' she asked outside. 'What's the point of going to see the film if you're going to walk out?'

Stephen grinned and looked up at Blair's name in the foyer. 'It's the only way I get to see her without making an appointment.'

Louise took that to be a reference to Bryn, Blair's agent. He had arrived earlier in the afternoon, wanting to see her about something. Stephen didn't like Bryn – 'slimy creep' was how he described him – but Louise was not sure that this aversion was enough to account for Stephen's odd behaviour.

'I can't stand that film,' he said, as they went to the car park. Dusk had fallen, it was almost dark.

'Why did you take me to see it, then?'

'To show you how awful it is.'

'Well, you haven't succeeded. I think it's good.'

'How can you say that, Louise?' Stephen said when they were in the car. 'All that nudity, the sex scenes, the girl is only fifteen. It's a paedophile's wet dream. It's obscene.'

Louise disagreed. 'I thought the nude scenes were artistic, beautiful even, and there's not that much sex. Besides, it's not gratuitous. It's part of the story.'

'Come on, Louise!' He rammed the car into gear. 'How would you feel if it was your sister up there? It's a jerk-off movie, pure and simple.'

'How would you feel if it wasn't?' Louise asked.

Headlights were coming on, engines revving. A couple of films had ended at the same time. They had to queue to leave.

'What?'

Louise repeated her question. 'How would you feel if it was another actress? Would you see the film differently?'

'That's not the point! She shouldn't be in that kind of movie.' Stephen cut into the line of traffic. 'I blame Gina and that slimeball Bryn. They're exploiting her.'

'Blair can make up her own mind, don't you think?'

'No,' Stephen answered, glancing up at the face on the giant poster. 'Sometimes she needs protecting from herself.'

Louise thought that Stephen would call it quits and take her back to Portland House but, when they reached the main road, he turned right, towards the city.

'Where are we going?' she asked.

'I've got to find a garage.'

The petrol gauge was on empty. There was a filling station up ahead. He pulled into the forecourt and cut the engine.

'Don't go anywhere,' he said, as he got out. 'I want to talk to you about something.'

While he was at the pump, Louise looked round for something to do. The engine was off, so no music. The map pocket contained just that. Maps. Louise reached to open the glove compartment. A slew of stuff fell onto her lap. Sunglasses, camera, mini binoculars, a flower, its frilled petals crushed and brown. A carnation, like the ones on the table in the pizza place. There were other things: photographs, bills, receipts, cards and coasters from restaurants and bars.

Louise scooped it all up, ready to stuff it back, when she stopped. She looked out of the window; Stephen was inside the garage, signing for petrol. Her fingers trembled as she checked through the collection. These things were like the ones that had been sent to Blair. Hands shaking, she tried to get them back into the compartment. There seemed too much now to fit the cramped space . . .

'Seen enough?' Stephen was getting back in; he reached over and slammed the flap shut.

Louise reached to open her door. Too late. Central locking whirred into place. Tyres squealed across the garage forecourt.

'Let me out!' The car was accelerating along a wide dual carriageway. 'Where are you taking me?'

'You'll see.'

Past the university signs, Stephen swung the car across two lanes of traffic, turning into a narrow lane with hedges each side. It was dark here. No street lighting. An island of blackness set in a sea of light.

'This is the part of town I was telling you about last night.' He brought the car to a stop, parking by a gate towards the end of Wheeler's Lane. 'I think it's time we had a little talk. You haven't exactly been straight with me, Louise. Have you?'

He wanted to know about Della. Who was she? What was she doing? Why had Blair employed her? He wanted to know about the conversation he had overheard on the extension. What gave her the right to harass his girlfriend, run checks on him?

'I'll tell you, shall I?'

Louise reached forward and opened the glove compartment.

'See these?' She pulled out a handful of items. 'Blair's been receiving things like this. No,' she corrected herself. 'Not like, Stephen. I'm talking *the same as*.'

'For example?'

'This cinema ticket.'

'What about it? I dropped into a multiplex. I thought I'd better see the film before I saw Blair.'

'The same day?'

He shrugged. 'I didn't know she was there . . .'

'What about these?' Louise spread the menus and coasters.

'It's just stuff I collect. I never sent it to anyone. This is from a place in London; Gina and Bryn took us for a meal. Hotel, bars . . .' he picked up the carnation, 'last night. I collect things. I've been doing it for years. Every now and then I sort through and stick them in a notebook. When I was at school – I was going through a bad patch – there was this counsellor – most of them were crap but this guy was OK. He suggested it, as a kind of therapy. A way to hang on to the good things and make sense of the bad things in your life.'

'That still doesn't account for these.' Louise held up the binoculars and the camera.

'The camera is there from London. The binoculars belong to Penny – she took them with her to the National Arena when she went to see some dance company. What is this, Louise? Do you think I've been spying, or something?'

Louise did not reply.

'You still haven't told me about Della,' Stephen said, overriding her silence. 'I think I'm owed some kind of explanation.'

'In that case, you better talk to your sister.

Blair employed her, not me. Why don't you ask her about it?'

But Stephen did not do that. Felicity met them at the door to tell him there had been an urgent call from Penny.

'She sounded very upset,' Felicity went on. 'I said you'd phone back. You can use my office. Thank goodness you're here,' she said to Louise when Stephen had gone off to make his call. 'Della's been so worried . . .'

'What about?'

'You, of course. And him.' Felicity nodded in the direction Stephen had gone. She passed her hand over her eyes. 'I wish I knew what was happening.'

'Why? What's the matter?'

Felicity's pale face was strained and tense. Her usual calm seemed to have deserted her.

'Blair and Gina have just had this massive row. Blair's very upset . . .'

'Where is she now?'

'Up in her room. I'll call Della, tell her you're back.'

'OK. I'll go and see Blair, try and calm her down.'

'Can I come in? It's me, Louise.'

'Yeah, as long as you don't bring any of the rest.'

'Like who?'

'Bryn, Gina, or Felicity.' Blair opened the door. 'They're driving me crazy. How was your evening with Stephen?'

'He's downstairs phoning his girlfriend.'

Blair raised an eyebrow and managed the ghost of a smile.

'That good, eh? It can't have been worse than here.' She threw herself on the bed. 'This place has been nightmare city. Every time I thought, "this cannot get worse", it did.'

'Why? What's been happening?'

'Felicity wants to bring the police in.'

'What does Della say?'

'That it's up to me.'

'What about Gina?'

'She's foaming at the thought of it. Wanted to leave, go to London – like *now.*'

'I thought it was Gina's idea to come here?'

'It was. But you know Gina. Logic not a strong point.'

'What did Della say about that?'

'She said, "Sudden changes of location will attract attention. We're talking about your daughter's safety here, not a shopping opportunity." ' Blair quoted, with the detective's tilt of the head, her laconic drawling voice. 'Gina demanded I sack her on the spot. We had a huge row.'

'Did you? Sack her, I mean?'

'Of course not. I want her on the case. Even if we leave.'

'When will that be?'

'Soon. But I won't be panicked into going right now. Hey!' She noticed her friend's expression. 'You're coming, too! I wouldn't leave without you.' Blair pushed heavy locks of hair back from her face. 'I hate what he's doing to me! He's getting in front of me! He's making me feel like I did when Gina used to drag me off to cheesy auditions in dodgy halls. It's as though he's watching, assessing and appraising, like the men I used to have to audition for. Some of them were truly reptilian. You would do your piece, curtsy and smile, and their eyes would be on you the whole time, completely cold and cruel.' Blair shivered, hugging herself. 'That's how I feel now – scared and small, like I'm ten years old and back on the circuit. I've got a feeling about this man,' she added. 'He's not any kind of besotted fan. He's something different.' She rocked as she spoke. 'Something else altogether.'

Chapter 16

Della had left Portland House to go straight to Penny Harbury's flat. Lights on upstairs indicated that the girl was in, even if she was not answering the door. The detective had not planned a return visit quite so soon, but the case was beginning to move, events were gaining their own momentum.

The lights went out. Della opened the door of her car. She would get one of the other tenants to let her in. If the girl had gone to bed, she would just have to get up again.

Della was just about to give the line of buzzers a random stab when the door opened.

'Oh, it's you,' Penny said, recognizing Della from earlier in the day. 'What's up? Did you leave something?'

'Not exactly.' Della blocked her way down the steps. 'I thought you didn't go out much.' She glanced at the package in the girl's hand. 'Funny time to be posting letters. Mind if I take a look?' She seized the jiffy bag, leaving the girl too astonished to object. 'Blair Paige, eh? You a fan, or something?'

'Sort of.'

'Mind if I open it?'

'Yes, I do! It's private!'

'So is what I have to discuss with you. Let's go back upstairs, shall we?'

*

'Let me introduce myself properly.' Della handed the girl a card. 'Della Rivers. Private detective.'

'I can read,' Penny said sarcastically.

She was trying for cool indifference, but her hand shook as she groped for the pack of cigarettes on her desk and lit one.

'Would you mind telling me what this package contains?'

'Yes, I would. Give it back to me!'

'Did you know,' Della continued, using the same chatty conversational tone, 'that it is now an offence, under the 1994 Criminal Justice Act, to harass another person with intent to cause alarm or offence?'

'What's that got to do with me? I want you to leave.'

Della tore the seal and shook the contents into her hand.

' "Definitive Blues Collection". Now why would you be sending that? Blair a blues fan, is she?'

Penny shook her head and turned away, refusing to reply.

'Stephen Franklin, your ex-boyfriend,' Della went on, 'is Blair's brother. Recently a large bouquet of roses was sent to her, paid for on his Barclaycard.'

'So?'

'Did you send them?'

'If they were ordered on his account, why don't you ask him?

'The florist says they were ordered by a

woman. This item also arrived recently.' Della took the first valentine out of her briefcase. 'Do you recognize it?'

'No. Should I?' Penny said, barely glancing at the card.

'Penny,' Della smiled, 'I know you sent it. There's a pile in your desk drawer just like it.'

'Maybe he sent that, too.'

'And these?'

Della took out some of the other items that had been sent to Blair.

'Why not?' Penny folded her arms, hugging herself. 'He collects all kinds of weird stuff.'

'But he didn't send it. You did.'

'I did not!' She paced the room, smoking in nervous snatches. 'So you can piss off, or I'll . . .'

'Call the police?' Della reached for the phone. 'Good idea. Not exactly 999. Let's try the local nick, shall we? I'll do it for you. Pass me the directory.'

Penny stopped halfway across the room, sitting down suddenly, as if her legs were no longer strong enough to carry her.

'OK. I sent the stuff. What are you going to do about it?'

'That depends.'

'On what?'

'What you tell me. Why did you do it?'

'I wanted to get back at him,' Penny said, sniffing back the tears that were beginning to sneak down her face. She stubbed her cigarette out viciously and tossed it into a half empty

Chinese food carton. 'He went to meet her at Heathrow . . .'

'Blair, you mean?'

'Yeah. He never goes anywhere with me, too much work, but it's like he'll drop everything, she just has to whistle. He stays with her in London at some big posh hotel and then he comes back and announces he'll be going to her place once she's settled and it's pretty clear I'm not invited. Not good enough for her, or her bloody snooty mother. We had a row. He walked out. After he'd gone, I just sat and cried, until I couldn't cry any more, and then I got to thinking how I could get even.'

She sniffed again and wiped her nose with the back of her hand; she was beginning to cry in earnest now. Della handed her a tissue from the box she carried for just such eventualities. Her gaze travelled over the girl's head to the wall behind her.

'Penny, tell me. Are you a dancer?'

'Wanted to be, at one time, but it didn't work out.' She looked up, puzzled by Della's change of tack, and then glanced back at the cabinet full of trophies and certificates. 'Oh, that. I put those there to please my mum. That's another thing we used to row about. Steve thought they were kitsch and stupid. Dance is my major.' She added, looking at Della, 'Those who can't, teach. That's what you're thinking, isn't it?'

Della shrugged. She was thinking about auditions. She was thinking about how for every

Blair Paige who made it, there were dozens, scores, hundreds, of little girls who didn't, who saw their own disappointment mirrored in their mothers' eyes, who went home in tears, hoping that next time it would be different, next time it would be them who got the part in *Annie*, or whatever. Over and over, again and again, until they grew too old, or too fat, or too tall, or finally realized they would just never be good enough and gave up altogether.

'Yeah. Well. I don't care what you think.' Penny blew her nose and began picking at the broken strands of Lycra whiskering her leggings. 'I sent them. After a couple of bottles of wine it seemed like a pretty good idea. I just scooped up what I could find from his London trip and posted it off. I wanted her to think someone was after her, watching her. If she thought it was Stephen so much the better. And then I remembered he'd said she didn't like roses, so I ordered a whole big bunch on his card. If anyone traced them it would look like he'd done that too, plus he'd have to pay and they cost a packet. It made me feel a whole lot better. I was really getting into it, but I was running out of things to send. I couldn't risk writing or phoning, then I remembered what happened to Amanda McCann . . .'

'Wait a minute. Who is Amanda McCann?' Della frowned. The name sounded familiar.

'She disappeared earlier this year,' Penny explained. 'They've just done a *Crimewatch* on her.'

'Oh, yeah. Right. Got her now. You knew her?'

'Amanda and I were on the same course.'

'You were friends?'

Penny shook her head. 'More acquaintances.'

'Did Stephen know her?'

She shook her head again. 'He'd met her, maybe once or twice, but we didn't mix much out of college.'

'I'm sorry, I still don't really understand . . .'

'Amanda got sent stuff by someone she didn't know. She used to tell me about it.'

'Like what? A CD?' Della held it up. 'Why blues?'

Penny shrugged. 'It's what got sent.'

'And what else? Flowers? That's what gave you the idea to send the roses?'

'Partly.'

'And the valentines?

'Valentines?' Penny looked up. 'I only sent one. The one you showed me.'

'You didn't send this?'

Della pulled the second valentine from her briefcase.

'I've never seen it before.'

'Are you sure?'

'Yes. Of course.'

She pushed the black card, with its rusty stained tissue-backed heart, back to Della.

'What about this?'

Della showed her the cinema ticket for *Degrees of Difficulty*. Penny read the message on the back.

'I didn't send that, either. I don't know any Louise.'

The girl looked up and their eyes met. They were both thinking the same thing: if she didn't send it, who did? The small amount of colour drained from Penny's face until the skin was tinged with grey.

'Are you all right?'

Della put her arm round the girl to support her. She was trembling. Della could feel the outline of her shoulder, the bones jutting sharp through her limp T-shirt.

'When did you last eat?' Della asked.

'I don't know. A couple of days. When I got that takeaway. Excuse me.'

Penny retched and bolted out of the room.

Della collected the aluminium boxes and emptied the rancid contents into the overflowing kitchen bin. She looked in the fridge. It contained something brown and squashy, that might once have been a lettuce, and half a tin of cat food.

'You shouldn't be on your own,' she said when Penny finally emerged from the bathroom. 'I'm going to phone Stephen.'

'No! Don't! He won't come!' The girl's eyes were huge; the very idea panicked her. 'Not after what I've done!'

'He will if he really cares about you.' Della picked up the phone. 'Here you are. If you don't talk to him, I will.'

*

Della had spoken to Felicity; Louise was safe and sound and Stephen had returned Penny's call. That little episode could go on hold, now she had another girl on her mind. Amanda McCann. The name repeated itself as she fumbled for the keys of her flat. It was too late to find out about her now. Getting more information would have to wait until the morning.

It had been a long day. She dropped her briefcase inside the door and stooped to pick up the mail. It was all junk stuff, apart from one white envelope. This was addressed to her, but just by name; it must have been hand delivered. Miss Della Rivers, in neat black printed capitals. Finepoint pen. Could be Rotring, could be anything. She was just about to open it when the phone rang.

'Hello. Della Rivers.'

'Hi, it's Mark.' He laughed at her lack of response. 'As in your brother. How are you doing, big sister?'

'Oh, hi.' Della sat down on the couch, kicked off her shoes and stretched her legs out. Why was he phoning this time of night? 'What can I do for you?'

'You phoned me, remember? You left a message,' he went on, getting no response. 'I've been trying to reach you all evening. Where have you been?'

'Out. Oh, I remember now. The swimming pool.'

'Swimming pool?'

'Yes. Jubilee Baths. 'You went there for coaching.'

'Yeah? What about it?'

'Do you remember a guy called Chris James.'

'Which one?'

'What do you mean, which one?' It was Della's turn to sound puzzled.

'There were two of them. Father and son.'

'Same names?'

'Yeah.'

'Didn't that get confusing?'

'Not really. We called the older one "Mr".'

'OK. Either. Both. Anything you recall.'

'Well . . . The old man was like the chief coach. He was very good, but tended to be a bit harsh and a bit partial.'

'He had favourites?'

Mark laughed again. 'Sort of. Let's put it this way, it helped if you were a girl. I didn't like him and he didn't like me – too much backchat. Once he got a down on you – it wasn't worth going. He was one of the reasons I left.'

'What about the other one, the son?'

'He seemed OK, he was popular, but I really didn't know him that well. He wasn't really a swimmer, more a diver. I remember watching him, he was brilliant, but his old man was tough on him, tougher on him than any of the rest, and he could be a real bastard. Make him dive until his ears were bleeding, taking the rip in front of the others. Word was, the old man could have been a contender, but didn't have the juice to make it, something like that, maybe that explains it. Della? Are you still there? Is that the kind of thing you wanted to know?'

'Yeah. Thanks, Mark. Bye for now.'

Della pressed the reset button and began to tap in numbers. It was time to call in a few favours.

'Is DI Ritchie there? Della Rivers. Yeah, I'll hold. In that case could you ask her to call me? Yes. It's urgent.'

Della called Nancy Lewis, a reporter at the *Post*, cradling the phone, as she chatted to the night duty bloke, so she could open the envelope. She slit the flap and quickly ended her call before tipping out the contents. The Queen of Swords, Marseilles Tarot pack, torn into confetti-size pieces, spilled across the table.

Chapter 17

The next morning Della arrived early at Portland House. She'd asked everyone to attend a brief meeting, to discuss developments, because the situation there was changing. She got to the PA's office to find even Gina subdued, sitting quietly, nervously plucking at her skirt. The strain was making lines on her face that cosmetics could not cover.

'Has anything else come?' Della asked.

Felicity shook her head. 'Not so far.'

'Good.' Della looked round. 'Where's Stephen?'

'He's gone to see Penny. He went after she phoned, last night . . .'

'At least he's done one thing right.'

'What do you mean?' Gina asked.

Della described her visit to the girl's flat.

'So it was her!' Gina's voice trembled. 'I never liked that girl. *Completely* wrong for Stephen—'

'She didn't send all of the things,' Della interrupted.

'Surely you don't think . . .' Gina stood up, vibrating with indignation. 'You *can't* think Stephen . . .'

She let the sentence dangle. The concluding phrase too awful to even utter.

'No. I don't think that.' If Della still had reservations about Blair's brother she was keeping them private. 'And I haven't finished. I'd like you to sit down.'

'Do as she says, Gina,' Blair said, quietly. 'OK, Della, what do you think we should do?'

'I still think we should leave,' Gina announced, before the detective could say anything, but her voice had lost some of its stridency.

Blair glared at her mother, but Della said, 'It's all right, Blair. I agree, as a matter of fact, but it's going to take careful planning.' The detective paced in front of them. 'We need to find somewhere safe for Blair to go. Security systems must be in place before she walks through the door. It can't be a known location, like her agent's flat – you can bet he knows about that – or a hotel. Too much unrestricted public access makes it impossible to guarantee protection.'

'I'm sure Bryn and I could organize something,' Gina suggested.

'OK.' The detective smiled at Gina, glad of her cooperation. It was vital they all worked together. 'That would be a big help.' She turned to Blair. 'We'll plan on getting you out of here by tomorrow, next day tops, as soon as a safe place can be found; meanwhile I want everything as normal as possible. What did you have planned?'

'I was going to take Louise to The Greswoldes. I have a session booked with Chris.'

'Go. Book a couple of the security guys in at the same time. But I'd be grateful if you took Felicity, not Louise.'

'Why?'

'I was hoping to borrow her. She could be a big help.'

Blair shrugged. 'If it's OK with her.' She looked over to her friend. 'What do you think, Louise? How do you fancy playing junior detective?'

'Yeah. Fine.' Louise was relieved. She had not been looking forward to another session in the gym.

Della turned to Felicity. 'What's on for tomorrow?'

'There's another round of publicity starting, follow-up to the film opening.' Felicity flicked through the diary. 'Interview in the afternoon with a journalist from one of the Sundays. Morning at *Pebble Mill,* appearance on *Lunch with Don and Jill.*'

'Cancel the journalist, but keep the telly. Last thing we want is a "Blair Paige Goes Into Hiding" story.'

'What about the police?' Felicity prompted.

'That's up to Blair.'

'What will they do?' Blair asked.

'Check with your security, run forensic checks on all items sent, mount extra patrols in the area, keep a watch on the house.' Della marked the procedures off on her fingers. 'You never know, he might think twice if he sees red and whites about. And they'll want to interview you, so you might have to cancel The Greswoldes.'

Blair looked at them focusing on her. The strain was beginning to tell on all of them. Especially Gina. She looked like she'd hardly slept. Anxiety haunted her mother's face, blunting her sharp blue gaze, lining her cheeks. She looked older, frail and afraid. Blair's heart suddenly went out to her. She took Gina's hand in hers and held it. They were mother and daughter after all. Despite what some of the bitchier gossip columnists said, their relationship was more than a business arrangement.

'OK,' she said. 'Go ahead. Call them in.'

'Right.' Della opened her briefcase and took out the items received. 'I'll leave these. I've removed the stuff Penny sent. If they need to talk to me or Louise, you have my numbers.'

Della left Felicity to contact the police. She beckoned for Louise, in a hurry now to leave. There was too much to do to spend all day briefing the local constabulary. If they wanted her, they would have to find her.

'What do you want me to do?' Louise asked. They were in Della's car now, heading for the city centre.

'I'm going to drop you off at the *Post* building. At reception ask for Nancy Lewis, she's expecting you. She'll take you down to their library archive. I want you to find all you can about these two girls.'

Della took a slip of paper from her pocket and gave it to Louise: *Amanda McCann and Heather Griffiths.*

'Why them?'

'They've both disappeared. Nancy has the dates. Be careful what you say to her. She's a good mate, but she's also a journalist, and a smart one. She'd shop her own granny if she thought there was a story in it.' Della pulled into a parking bay in front of the newspaper building. 'If she asks you about the case, just tell her I'm looking for a teenage runaway.'

'Where are you going?'

'I'm going to Edgely.'

'Back to the office?'

'No. I'm going to where Amanda lived, see what I can find out.'

Louise sat in a booth in the archive office, going back through newspaper stories. She began with Amanda McCann, the most recent girl to disappear, making notes as she scanned the pages. Amanda McCann had gone missing in March of this year. The first story, 'Student Disappears', was a front-page headline. Louise read down the column of print next to a colour photo of a pretty dark-haired girl. In subsequent editions, the story slipped from the front to the inside pages. 'Amanda: Search Continues' turned into 'Concern Grows For Missing Student'. The stories ended with 'Police Still Baffled', dated 21st March, a week after her disappearance.

Louise looked over her notes. Amanda had been reported missing after she failed to return home from the University. Her bicycle had turned up on a housing estate on the other side of the city, with some kid riding it; the serial number matched that of Amanda's bike. The student's route home was checked again and again, but no one had seen anything. A fingertip search of Wheeler's Lane discovered nothing. The hunt for clues widened to the woods and fields either side, but no evidence was found. No clues meant no news, no more story.

Louise switched to microfilm to look for the other girl on her list, Heather Griffiths. She had to go back nearly four years, but this had been a bigger story. Heather was younger, just fifteen, and had disappeared the day after Valentine's Day – the press had dubbed her 'Valentine Girl'; that was the headline which had lodged in Della's mind. Louise read through story after story. In some ways she found this more upsetting.

Heather had left the local leisure centre after swimming practice and had not been seen since. There was a picture of her; again she was dark-haired and pretty. No, that was wrong. Louise brought the photo up bigger. Even allowing for distortion, and the blurred black and white, it was easy to see that this girl was beautiful. What affected Louise most were the appeals from her parents, anguished, pleading, alternating between hope and despair. The photographs of them showed an oldish couple. Heather was their only child; they were willing to air their private grief in the slight hope that someone who had seen something might take pity on them. Their plight brought in extra information. A girl, fitting Heather's description, had been seen talking to a man, getting into his car. But the sightings were vague on detail. It was dark and the witnesses were too far away to make any positive identification.

Louise pressed the button on the machine, whizzing the pages on, but even this story dried up eventually.

'I think that's it. There won't be anything else unless they find a body.'

Louise turned to find Nancy Lewis standing looking down at her. Hazel eyes, light and amused, appraised her from behind outsize horn-rimmed glasses. Nancy was in her mid-twenties, small and slight, dressed in a T-shirt and a long floral skirt. Strands of flaming red hair floated out to frame her pale freckled face; the various clips and grips she used to keep it back seemed to have given up the struggle.

'I had a dig through a file upstairs and came up with another name. Kay Walsh. She went missing about a year ago.' Nancy's byline had been on most of the stories Louise had been reading. The reporter kept a file on missing girls, hoping to use it for a feature. 'I've photocopied my notes.' She held up a folder. 'Della's welcome to these, too. Where is she?'

'I don't know. Gone off to see someone.'

Nancy grinned. 'Left you to do the boring stuff, eh? Still, if the cat's away . . .' She winked. 'Fancy a drink? I'm gasping.'

Chapter 18

The house Amanda McCann had shared was on a newish estate a few miles west of the university. A tall blonde girl, dressed for tennis, was coming out of the front door. She was carrying a sports bag, a vacuum tube of Wilson balls and a racket case.

'Excuse me.' Della walked up the short drive. 'Are you Mary Spencer? Is this your house?'

The young woman nodded.

'Do you mind if I ask you a few questions?'

'I'm in a bit of a rush . . .' Mary's tone and expression were less than enthusiastic.

'It won't take long. Did Amanda McCann live here?'

'Yes, she did, as a matter of fact.' She didn't look very surprised at being asked a question like that, but her pale grey eyes narrowed and her sunburnt freckled face grew suspicious, guarded. 'Why do you want to know? Are you a reporter?'

'No.' Della took out her card. 'Private detective.'

'Well,' she looked at her watch, 'I'm off to play tennis.'

Della moved closer, blocking her way to the car. 'Just a couple of minutes . . .'

'OK.' She glanced up and down the quiet suburban road. 'You'd better come inside. But make it quick. I'm due on court.'

The hall was cool after the heat outside, and free of clutter. Laura Ashley wallpaper. Neutral colours.

'What do you want to know?'

Mary Spencer listened as Della, careful to mention no names, explained the case she was currently engaged in.

'Did Amanda get anything like that at all?' she asked, watching to see the effect. 'Unwanted phone calls, items through the mail, unsolicited letters?'

'Well . . .'

Mary hesitated. Della waited. In the silence between them, Mary weighed it up. The police had instructed her not to talk about this aspect of the case. But she was in a hurry and this woman looked as though she'd stand here all day if necessary.

'I was told not to say . . . but . . . yes, she did.'

'Like what?' Della flicked open her notebook.

'Oh, flowers, cards, I don't know what. Amanda threw most of it away. The police have the rest. Perhaps you ought to talk to them.'

'Maybe I will. But right now I'm talking to you. Are her things still here?'

'Her parents were supposed to come and pick them up but they haven't yet.' She shrugged. 'Couldn't face it, I guess.'

'Can I see her room?'

'Oh, I've let that. Couldn't afford not to. Her stuff's in the garage.'

'Can I take a look?'

'What for? The police have already been through it . . .'

'They might have missed something.' Della folded her arms. 'I thought you were a friend of hers. Don't you want to know what happened to her?'

'Of course I do.' Mary bit her lip, the reserve she'd been showing starting to break down. 'Sorry. I'm not being very helpful. D'you think these cases, yours and Amanda's, might be connected?'

'Could be.' It was the detective's turn to be guarded.

'In that case, you're welcome to look through her things.' She glanced at the clock. 'It's just I'm running late . . .'

'You don't have to stay. Here.' Della handed her a business card. 'Take this. Anything damaged, missing, I'll accept full liability.'

'OK.' Mary took it and led the way back outside. 'Here's the key. Pop it through the front door when you've finished.'

Della rolled up the garage door. Across the gritty stained concrete floor, a pile of belongings was stacked up against the far wall. Books, files, cuddly toys. A shiver, tiny ice needles running down the spine. Amanda McCann's life packed into boxes.

Della's old CID training took over. Build a picture of the subject: interests, hobbies, personality. Methodical, painstaking, go through everything, bit by bit, looking for the part that does not fit. She pulled the first box to her. The hard plastic rattle of tape cassettes.

'Found anything?'

Della turned, surprised by the voice behind her. She'd lost track of time. Mary might have played a couple of matches by now, or she might not have fancied a total stranger rummaging about in her garage and doubled straight back.

'Just this.'

It was a CD. A blues compilation, similar to the one Penny had planned to send. Similiar, but not the same. These were original tracks from the archives, re-recorded and digitalized.

'It's a compact disc.' Mary's eyebrows drew together as if to say: *Do they pay detectives for that?*

'Yes. But it's the only one. The rest are cassettes. And it doesn't fit. The other stuff is mostly dance.' She pushed the box with her foot. 'Rave, techno – that kind of thing.'

Mary stared at the CD cover. *King Blues,* in pale turquoise letters over a sepia photograph of a Chicago blues man, trilby in one hand, guitar on his lap. A black velvet hairband was stretched round the plastic shell.

'The CD's not mine and Amanda certainly wouldn't have bought it. She didn't like that kind of music. That hair thing could be hers, though. She used to wear them when she tied her hair back. What's it doing on there?'

Dells shrugged noncommittally. 'Perhaps the

case is broken, or something. Could she have been sent this?'

'Possibly . . . Hang on – can I see it for a minute?'

'Sure. But hold the corners, there could still be prints.'

'There is one thing. Just before she disappeared there was one of those "Our Tune" features on the radio. For some reason Amanda thought it was about her. Rest of us thought it was a bit of a laugh, but it really upset her.'

'You don't know why?'

'No. But it was Blues. I remember that.' Mary frowned, nose wrinkling at the artists' obscurity. 'I don't think it was any of these. I can hardly see them getting airtime.'

'Which one was it?'

Mary shrugged. 'They all sound the same to me.'

'I meant which station.'

'Oh, I don't know. Probably local. Amanda reckoned they played better stuff, but I haven't a clue which one. She'd tune into anything – follow the music.'

'Do you mind if I take it?'

'Help yourself.'

'Thanks.' Della dropped the CD into her pocket. 'If you remember anything else . . .'

'I've got your card.'

'Tell me, Mary,' Della said as they stood looking down at the compacted life of Amanda McCann, 'do you think she did a runner? Were things getting too much, getting on top of her?'

'No.' The girl's blonde ponytail swung in emphatic denial. 'I don't think that.'

'Why not?'

'She had no reason. She was a popular girl, lots of friends, boyfriend, no problems there. She was doing really well on her course. She was happy. Everything was going right. And then there's her bike . . .'

'Her bike? What about it?'

'They picked a kid up riding it. Amanda would never have left that. It's a Cannongate, worth more than most students' cars. She wouldn't even put it in the bike racks, used to leave it in the porters' office.' She paused. 'I'm sorry if I was a bit offhand when you first arrived. It's just, I'm sick of answering questions and then no one doing anything. The police haven't been round for ages. It's like they don't care any more, like they've given up.' She turned to Della, unshed tears in the corners of her grey eyes. 'I hope you find something.'

'So do I. If you remember anything else, give me a call.'

'Of course. I'll be in touch.'

'That's better.' Nancy put down her glass. 'Hot, isn't it? We'll be dusting off "Pets in Parked Car Peril" and "Phew, What a Scorcher!" if this goes on.' Her eyes narrowed as she viewed the concrete piazza baking away outside the café-bar. 'Now, tell me, Louise, what are you doing with Della? If you don't mind me saying so, you look awfully young to be a detective.'

Nancy took another sip from her drink. Her greeny fawn eyes, magnified by the spectacle lenses, returned to smile at Louise. Behind her teasing gaze was a penetrating curiosity.

'I did my work experience with FemTec,' Louise replied. 'And they've given me a job for the summer – helping Janine.'

'FemTec.' Nancy pulled a face. 'I'm not entirely convinced about the name, to be honest. Sounds like some kind of panty shield, but I like the card, very flash.' She fished one out of her T-shirt pocket and brushed it against the other hand. 'I heard Della's pulled a big-time prestige client – you know anything about that?'

'Me?' Louise shook her head. 'No. Nothing. What makes you think that?'

'Just a whisper from one of the law court guys. Wendy couldn't contain herself. Wouldn't say who it was, though. Sure you don't know?'

'No idea. Sorry.'

'So,' Nancy lit a cigarette, 'what is she working on?'

The reporter's shrewd eyes were on her again, observing her through the smoke, gauging, assessing, hungry for a story. Journalists were good sources of information but they had to be treated with the utmost caution. Remembering Della's warning, Louise spun the line she'd been given about a teenage runaway and a pair of anxious parents.

Nancy believed her. Maybe Wendy was keeping the tasty clients for herself, leaving Della with the everyday stuff. The case Louise was describing was just the kind that ended up with a private detective.

'People disappear every day.' Nancy tapped her ash. 'There's usually a reason, if you dig deep enough – abuse, debts, drugs, trouble at home, with the boyfriend. Often they turn up after a couple of weeks – even if they don't, interest soon drops to zero, even as far as the police are concerned, unless they find a body. They don't have the manpower to go chasing runaways.'

'Do you think these girls ran away?' Louise asked, indicating the file Nancy had brought with them.

'Could have done. If they have, it's a hell of a job to find 'em. Most end up on the game in London, or somewhere.'

'Even a girl like Heather Griffiths?'

'Yes.' Nancy stubbed out her cigarette. 'Even a nice girl like that. If the kid's done a runner, Della's work is cut out.'

'How do you know her?' Louise asked, steering away from the fictional case.

Nancy smiled. 'Della? We go back quite a while. She started on the force the same time I started on the paper.'

'Why did she leave? The police, I mean?'

'Don't you know?'

Louise shook her head.

'In that case, maybe you'd better ask her.' Nancy paused, but she was not known for discretion and it was an excellent story. 'She had a scene with one of her male colleagues, Jack Ryder. They were on a training course, there was a party at the end of it, and he thought he'd pulled her. He went back to her room, but Della wasn't in the mood. I don't know what happened, but she accused him of sexual harassment and he ended up with a broken nose and a fractured cheekbone. Her senior officers tried to hush it up, but Della wasn't having any. If he wasn't disciplined, she'd bring charges. He countered with assault.' Nancy shook her head. 'It was so stupid; they'd been seeing each other on and off, but this must have been during an "off" period. Anyway, Della wouldn't back down. When it was clear she wasn't going to get anywhere, she resigned. Quit the force. End of promising career. She'd have made inspector by now if she'd stayed in, like her mate, Helen Ritchie.'

'Who would have? Gossiping about me again? Don't believe a word this woman tells you.'

'Hi, Della.' Nancy looked up. 'Got this for you.' She waved her folder of photocopied notes. 'Do you want a drink?'

'Yes, OK. Coffee.'

Della sat down and opened the file as the waiter brought her double espresso. On top was a list of young women, between the ages of fifteen and thirty, who had been reported missing over the last five years. A long list, but Nancy had done her homework. Thick smudged highlighter marked disappearances thought to be particularly baffling or suspicious. Girls with no reason to run. Not in care, or any kind of trouble. No previous, no history of abuse, drugs, incest. No problems at home, work, school. No preparations before and no contact since. They had simply vanished. Listed in reverse order of disappearance: *Amanda McCann, Kay Walsh, Heather Griffiths*.

'Who's this Kay Walsh?' Della looked over to Nancy.

'Estate agent's clerk, disappeared about a year ago.' The reporter shrugged. 'I couldn't dig up much on her, I'm afraid.'

'We'd better go.' Della drained her cup. 'Thanks, Nance.'

'Any time.' The reporter smiled. 'I hope you find her.'

'Who?' Della asked.

'The kid you're looking for.'

'Oh. So do I. Thanks again, Nancy. See you.'

Della's on to something, the reporter thought as she watched them go. She could smell it. What did they call the press? Hyenas? Hyenas could force a lioness off her kill, she'd seen it in a documentary the other day. She raised her glass as Louise turned to wave. That went for cubs as well.

Chapter 19

'Are we going back to Portland House?' Louise asked when they got in the car.

'Not just yet,' Della said. Louise sat back, relieved. She liked doing this. 'We'll try that Leisure Centre where Heather G was last seen. We need to go into these girls' lives, see what we can find.'

Stoke Park Sports and Leisure Centre was slightly out of town, part of a big greenfield development, near to the multiplex cinema where Louise had seen Blair's film the night before.

'Nancy's notes say Heather received flowers and stuff through the post before she disappeared,' Della was saying as she drove into the car park. 'This seems to be a factor linking all the girls. When you look at a number of cases with similarities the first one can reveal more than all the others put together. The first time tends to be less planned,' she added, parking the car, 'more likely to be on impulse, targeting someone known to them, someone they see regularly.'

'What if she's not the first, though?' Louise said as they went to the entrance. 'There could have been others before . . .'

'Heather's the first one we know of. We've got to start somewhere, haven't we?' Della pushed open the heavy plate-glass doors. 'And here's as good a place as any. Excuse me . . .'

'Two adult swims? Three pounds ninety, please.' The woman behind the till was already dispensing the tickets.

'I haven't come to swim,' Della replied. 'I would like to see the manager.'

Martin Halifax, who now managed the complex, had not been working there at the time of Heather Griffiths' disappearance, but he insisted on showing them round. They finished the tour in the spectator gallery so they could fully appreciate the Olympic-sized main pool, the smaller irregularly shaped novelty leisure area, the flume and wave machine. It was hot here, humid. The pool was crowded, choppy with activity.

'Can we go somewhere else?' Della could hardly hear herself speak.

'Of course. Follow me.'

The din receded, as they went through a series of swinging doors, but faint cries were still audible, even in his office.

'I wasn't working here at that time,' he said. 'They had a temporary chap in, luckily. I couldn't start till April.'

'Why luckily?'

'Bad publicity! What with that, and teething troubles with the flume, cast a blight – receipts were down for the whole post-Christmas period.'

'When did this place open?' Della pulled out her notebook.

'September of the year before. But it wasn't fully operational until Christmas. I don't think I'm being much help.' He swivelled in his chair. 'I'm trying to think who might have been here – we do get a high staff turnover. You could ask Annie; she's been around a while, she might remember.'

'Thanks. And where can we find her?'

'Reception, probably. Or in the back office.'

'Thanks for your help.'

'Not at all. I've never talked to a real live detective before. Come back on an adult swim night,' he winked as he showed them to the door. 'I'll arrange a couple of complimentaries.'

Annie Kelley was still inside her booth dispensing tickets. Della waited until the queue had died down before asking if she wouldn't mind answering a few questions.

''Course not, love,' she replied from behind her glass wall. 'If Tracey won't mind standing in. Tracey!'

A girl emerged from an office behind the ticket booth. She groaned at Annie's request but agreed to take her place. The older woman hopped off her high stool and beckoned them through a door in the panelled wall. She was small and dumpy with a cap of iron-grey curls and thick-lensed spectacles. She wore roughly the same uniform as the other staff, but did not exactly look the part. Maybe she was there to give the overweight older punters some encouragement.

'This won't take long,' Della said. 'Is there anywhere we can talk?'

Annie led them through to a small room she called the office.

'Fancy a brew?' she asked as she flicked the kettle on.

They were in some kind of staffroom. Easy chairs stood next to a desk piled with leaflets and papers, a lost property bin spilling bits of kit, and a battered green filing cabinet. There was a partially filled-in year planner and a whiteboard covered with scribbled messages and duty rosters. Along the other wall was a line of photographs of swimming teams which spanned a good many years, judging by the differing styles in swimwear and the change from colour to black and white.

'What do you want to know?' Annie asked as she poured boiling water into a battered aluminium teapot.

'Were you working here when Heather Griffiths disappeared?'

The same question, precise and direct, had far more of an impact on Annie than it had done on her boss. Her arm shook as she replaced the kettle and, at the mention of the girl's name, her jovial good-natured face crumpled into sadness.

'I certainly was. Terrible business. Such a nice kiddie. I know her family. They still haven't got over it, don't reckon they ever will; Heather was an only one, see? Her mum keeps her room ready, thinking she's going to turn up, but I don't know so much. She didn't strike me as the kind to run away, not at all that type.'

'Why do you say that?'

'She was pretty enough, but young for her age, still a child in lots of ways. Didn't gossip and eye up the lads like the others.'

'Any mention of boyfriends?'

'Not that I heard. Quite a little homebody. Loved her mum and dad. Lived for her swimming. She was very dedicated, never missed a practice. That's her, up there.' She pointed up to the swimming teams. 'Middle of the third row. She was captain. There was talk of her training with the England squad . . .'

While Annie went on to describe Heather's swimming career, what she'd achieved, what might have been, Louise walked over to take a look at the team photographs. People don't look their best in swimming photos, hair half dry, skin winter pale against dark team costumes. The lighting inside a pool is hardly flattering, either, but Louise was struck again by Heather's good looks. A dark-haired girl with regular features and a wide smile, even in that bleached light you could see the triumph shining from her grey eyes. In the middle, clutching the cup, her team-mates all around, she looked very happy.

The man standing with them, dressed in tracksuit top and shorts, must be the coach. Louise's attention was already beginning to switch away from him, back to Annie and Della, when something made her stop and look again. She knew that face. Going up to the photo, tracing the names underneath, she found the one she was looking for.

'Della. Come here a minute,' she said, cutting into the conversation going on behind her. 'Take a look at this.'

The image was fuzzy, like he'd moved or something, but it did look like him. Sporting a moustache he had since shaved off, his hair longer, cut in a different style, he had the same large dark eyes and the same half-smile.

Annie came over and peered up, curious to see what had taken their attention away from the missing girl.

'That's Chris James.' She pointed with a stubby finger. 'He was the coach. He was that chuffed with them. You can see on the photograph.' She smiled for a moment and then turned away to polish her misting spectacles. 'One of the best teams he'd ever had. And he'd run more than you've had hot dinners.'

This was an under-15 team. The photograph had been taken at least a year before Heather disappeared. Della followed the team photos along the wall. Most of them were black and white. The coach was the same in each one, standing against the wall, to the side of the bunched groups of swimmers, hands behind his back, staring straight out. The dates went way back. The Chris James she knew would have been a boy. Then she remembered her brother saying, 'We called him "Mr".' This must be the father.

'How do you know Chris, then?' Annie was asking.

'Oh, er, through a client of mine. But I think . . .'

'Chris coached the teams for years. That was taken down at the old pool, not here,' Annie went on. The photographs were all taken against the chequered tiling of a municipal baths. 'He didn't make the move with the rest of us.' She shook her head. 'I can't really imagine him anywhere else but Jubilee. He put years into them old baths. Trained there himself when he was a kid. I didn't know him then but they say he could have been in the Olympics. Back in the sixties. I don't know the full story, but something happened meant he couldn't go. Coached some world-class swimmers, though.'

'I think I met his son, actually,' Della cut in, to stop any further misunderstanding.

'Young Chris? A nice lad. Done well, considering, going to college and everything. I wish my two were more like him.'

'Why "considering"?'

'Soon after this place opened his dad was took bad . . .'

'Like how? Did he have a stroke or something?'

'No. Nothing like that. More of a breakdown. Chris gave up his chance to go away to university. He changed to the local tech to be near his dad.'

Annie glanced at the clock on the wall. 'Is that all? I mean, I'd like to chat, but I ought to be getting back.'

'One more question. Is there a Mrs James, at all?'

'I suppose she's somewhere, but not with him. She went off with another man, left when Chris was a little lad. Some might think his dad was a bit heavy handed, too strict, but bringing a kid up on your own isn't easy. It hasn't done him any harm, as far as I can see.'

'Just one other thing. Chris James Senior was not working here when Heather disappeared.'

'No, Bob Travis took over. Management wanted someone younger.'

'I see. Do you know what Mr James is doing now?'

'Last time I heard, he was working up at the university.'

'In the sports centre?'

'No. Nothing like that. Security.'

'A bit of a comedown, isn't it?'

Annie looked puzzled.

'From managing a swimming pool?'

Annie laughed. 'That's a good one! Bless you, my love.' She wiped her eyes. 'He was coach, and a bit of everything else besides, from tickets to poolside, but he weren't no manager!'

'Excuse me.'

Louise and Della both turned to see the girl, Tracey, running towards them.

'You were talking about Heather,' she said, catching up.

'Did you know her, too?' Della asked.

'I was at school with her. We used to have swimming on the same nights. I was never as good as her, but we trained together so I knew her pretty well. It's just, the thing is . . .'

'What?'

'Well, I heard Annie say, you know, what a good girl she was – no boyfriends, butter wouldn't melt . . .'

Della's hand froze halfway to her car keys.

'And that wasn't so?'

'Well, not strictly. I mean, she's right in one way, Heather didn't bother with boys her own age, but she was seeing someone. I reckon he sent her them things, the valentines and that lot. She said she didn't know who they were from. At least, that's what she told her mum, but I reckon she did.'

'Did she tell you? Confide in you?'

The girl shook her head. 'No. She was dead secretive. But like she got this tape, right? She played it on her walkman.'

'Tape? What of?'

'Sixties stuff. Not Soul, the other stuff.'

'Blues?'

'Yeah. I got the idea that this guy was older than her and she didn't know how to deal with it. Like she was out of her depth, in over her head. That last night, after training, she made a real effort, drying her hair properly, putting on make-up. I reckoned she was off to meet someone. Like, we usually went home together – but that night we never. She said her dad was picking her up, but it weren't true.'

'You told the police this?'

'Oh, yeah,' Tracey nodded, 'but you was talking to Annie, and I didn't want you to get the wrong idea.'

'Thanks, Tracey.'

'Glad to help. I've never talked to a detective before. What are you doing?'

'Looking for a girl.'

'Like Heather?'

'Kind of.'

'Well, I better be getting back. Good luck.'

'Thanks.'

Della looked at her watch. Her appointment with DI Helen Ritchie wasn't for another hour. Time for one more stop before she dropped Louise off and went to call in a few favours.

They drove away from the out-of-town development, back along the Western Road. It funnelled down from dual carriageway to crowded streets of little shops and restaurants.

'Why are we going this way?' Louise asked, looking out of the window as the car slowed in the crawling congestion.

'Call it a nostalgia trip.' Della took the next left turn. 'There's the old baths.' She stopped the car. 'Not much like the nice new Leisure Centre. Did you ever go there?'

Louise nodded. 'Once or twice. Brownie Swimming Galas.'

'I spent a lot of time there when I was a kid. I used to drop in once in a while when I was in the force. It was old-fashioned, but at least it was built for swimming, not messing about in. It used to be a really nice place. You wouldn't think so now, would you?'

'MUNICIPAL BATHS' stood out in carved stone relief on red brick streaked and blackened by city grime. Most of the urban nouveau façade was boarded up with splintering fly-postered plywood. Buddleia bushes, purple spears just breaking into flower, sprouted out from behind the rusty iron railings.

'It's very big.'

'It was a real baths, you know, for people who didn't have ones at home. You could go and book a cubicle, bath, soap, towel, everything.' Della laughed. 'I didn't like those. They were really creepy.' She told Louise the dead tramp story. 'Still, better get on.' Della started the car. 'I'll drop you back at Blair's and then go and meet Helen—'

'You can't get out down the bottom now, love.' A man called from the open door of a small works. *Benfield & Sons. Forgers & Stampers.* Della waved her thanks and turned back to the main road. He returned her salute and went into the heat and clang of heavy machinery.

Chapter 20

During Louise's absence, the police had been and gone; they would interview her in the morning. Bryn had been scouring London for a new address. Gina's brief was exacting, but he had come up with something. Gina would go the next day to view it; if she approved they would be moving.

Louise spent the evening with Felicity. Gina had taken the whole family out to dinner, including Stephen's girlfriend. The celebration was her mother's idea; Blair suggested inviting Penny. At first, Stephen would not even discuss it, but Blair talked him round and booked a table for four at an expensive place recommended by Bryn.

'I'd rather be here, personally,' Felicity said, neatly spearing a section of beans on toast. 'Eating this.'

'How do you mean?'

Felicity put down her fork and touched her napkin to her mouth.

'Dinner with the Family Grim. I pity that Penny. I wonder how long Gina is going to carry on pretending they all get on so famously. When is she going to wake up to the fact that you can't ignore one child, put him in boarding school, while you take the other one halfway round the world to make you a fortune, and then expect everything to be fine. Tell me something, Louise – do you hear any mention of their father?'

'I remember him OK,' Louise frowned, 'but no one's said much since I've been here. Except Stephen.'

'What did he say?'

'Said his dad didn't care about him, either.'

'Exactly. And he might as well have disappeared altogether as far as Blair's concerned. She's only got Gina, who has to be one of the most selfish people I've ever met. I don't know which one I feel most sorry for, to be honest, but it's no use pretending they can get on as a family. I mean, I like him and all that, but I think it's better that Stephen's not here.'

'They seemed all right to me,' Louise countered. 'They seemed happy enough to see each other.'

'Maybe. But how long will it stay like that? It's not her – it's him.' Felicity pushed her plate away. 'There's a lot going on under the surface. You've seen how he is around Blair; he doesn't know what he feels, how to treat her. If he stayed much longer, he'd only upset her. After what Gina's done to him it's a wonder he can form any relationships at all – look at the mess he's made with that girl.'

Louise could not find an answer to that and was rather relieved when a rapping on the door cut their conversation short. A man was standing the other side of the reflecting glass. It was dark outside; night had fallen.

'Are you expecting anyone?' Louise asked.

'No . . .' Felicity jumped down from her stool and went over, peering through the double glazing. 'It's all right. It's only Chris.' Tumblers clicked as she turned the key. 'Come in.'

'I was just out for a run. Saw the light, thought I'd drop by. Hi, Louise,' he added as he noticed her.

'Do you want a beer or something?' Felicity asked.

He said 'no' to the beer but accepted a mineral water.

'Any particular kind?' Felicity's voice came from inside the fridge now. 'Evian, Perrier, Volvic?'

'I don't mind. Whichever.' He took the bottle from Felicity and drank straight from it. 'That's better,' he said, placing the empty container on the counter. 'Blair around?'

Felicity shook her head. 'She's gone out to dinner with Gina.'

'I just wondered what happened today. Why the session was cancelled.'

'We've had the police here,' Felicity explained. 'There's been an escalation in tension. Blair agreed to call them.'

'She'll just have to work extra-hard tomorrow morning.'

'What do you mean?'

'Her morning run.'

'She won't be doing it, I'm afraid.' Felicity

smiled an apology. 'She has appointments all morning.'

'OK. Have to be the next day.'

'We might not be here. We're leaving. Didn't you know?'

'No.' His eyes had widened slightly at her words, his head jerking as if he had received a physical blow. A muscle jumped in his cheek as he added, 'First I've heard about it.'

'Oh, Chris, I'm really sorry . . .' Felicity apologized again, contrite on Blair's behalf. 'It's most remiss of us. Of course the move was not confirmed until late this afternoon. I'm sure she planned to tell you. Maybe we can re-arrange her schedule to fit a session in . . .'

'Yeah.' Chris gave a tight smile. 'Maybe. I will have that beer, if it's still on offer.'

He sat down on a stool opposite Louise, while Felicity went to get his beer. His mouth smiled but his dark brown eyes smouldered, as if the insulting slight was burning its way deep inside.

'What were you doing today?' he asked Louise.

'I was helping Della, Della Rivers.'

'Junior detective, eh?'

'Not exactly. More research. Into missing girls.'

'Like Heather?'

'Heather Griffiths? How did you know . . .'

'Your boss asked me about her.'

'So you knew her?'

'Yes I did. Very talented swimmer. Would have

made the national squad if she hadn't disappeared.'

'What do you think happened?' Louise asked, thinking over her conversation with Nancy. 'Could she have run away?'

'She was one of my Dad's protégées,' he laughed mirthlessly and harsh, 'so it is a possibility. Although he was nice to her, if memory serves. Who knows?' He spread his palms. 'It's difficult to tell what's in someone else's head, even if you know them well and, as I told your boss, I hardly knew her. Swimming at that level is a pressure thing,' he added, smoothing the skin by the sides of his mouth. 'A punishing physical schedule, training every day, no time for a life outside. And there's other other kinds of pressure. To win, to be the best. Some kids can't stand it. They crack, want out. Cheers.' He accepted the beer. 'You've got to want it for yourself. Not someone else. That's one of the things I try to teach the kids I coach. Don't let anybody live through you.'

'What do you mean?' Felicity asked.

'I get kids, sportsmen, and women, who are under such pressure to achieve. People don't understand, you've got to encourage, not criticize – and having to carry someone else's hopes and dreams acts like an invisible handicap. It isn't just talent, or any particular kind of sport, athletics, swimming, boxing, doesn't matter. There's a point where a parent has to back off, or the kid will crack up or get out.'

He's talking about himself, Louise thought, *he's not talking about anybody else.*

'Were you a swimmer?'

'Diver.' He corrected her.

'Of course, how stupid of me.'

'Used to dive in competition. Won medals. Want to see?'

'But you don't compete now. What happened?'

He laughed. 'Too old for a start! When I got to national level, I started getting problems and had to give up.'

'Were you disappointed?'

'Sure. At the time. But not any more. I'm happier teaching other people than doing it myself.'

He drained his beer and stared into the half-distance, looking back to a world of shivering pools and shattered dreams where a fingertip out of line meant the difference between failure and victory.

'Would you like another?' Felicity nodded towards the empty bottle.

'No, I'd better get going.' He stood, ready to leave. 'What's the matter?'

They both turned to Louise. Her sharp gasp and startled look nearly made Felicity drop the glass she was holding.

'What is it?'

'I thought I saw something.'

Louise was staring into the darkness beyond the bright kitchen.

'Where?'

Chris James turned round to confront his mirrored self.

'Out there. Just now. When you stood up. I thought there was someone outside.'

It was probably a trick of the light but, for a moment, it had seemed as though his image, reflected in the plate glass, had taken a sidestep to the right, breaking away from itself.

'Are you sure?' Felicity went up to the window.

'Could be Roy,' Chris said. 'We had a chat as I came up.'

'Could be,' Louise said, doubtfully. Roy's uniform was dark, and the figure she saw had been wearing something light.

'There.' Felicity pulled the blind, shutting out the night. 'I'll have a word with Blair about the run.'

'Yeah, you do that.' Chris stepped into the darkness. 'It could be our last one.'

Chapter 21

Della's friend, Helen Ritchie, had agreed to get the police files on the missing girls, but acquiring and photocopying them had taken time. They arranged to meet for an evening drink, selecting a city wine bar, too upmarket for most of Helen's police colleagues. Then Jack Ryder came in.

'Hi, Della. How's it going? Still chasing errant husbands?' he said, with a sardonic grin. 'Isn't this cosy?' He put a hand on the backs of their chairs. 'Quite a little reunion. Can I join in?'

Helen waved an invitation for him to sit down.

'Go on, seriously, what are you working on?' he said to Della as he helped himself to a glass of wine.

'I can't discuss it. Client confidentiality.'

'Client confidentiality!' Jack's laughter rang round the bar. 'That's what I love about you, Della. You can still make me laugh!'

He drained his glass and moved on, but the transfer of files had taken place in the ladies'. Della stayed for another drink and did not make it back to her flat until past midnight.

She made a pot of coffee and got down to work, clearing her desk, setting out a fresh yellow pad, finepoint pen, and propelling pencil. The police files were in the order in which she intended to view them: Kay first, least known about her; then Amanda; and finally Heather, the thickest file.

She opened the brown manila folder with 'Kay Walsh' on it. Receiving officer's report, statements from employer, fellow employees, neighbours. Kay did not appear to have friends. She lived alone. Her flat had been entered, searched, nothing found. One set of prints throughout – belonging to the girl.

Della took notes. Kay was 24 years old at the time of her disappearance in May last year, older than the other two girls. The initial report had been filed by the owner of BodySmiths Gym and Health Club. Kay had been a regular, apparently, but she had not been in for nearly a week. Della looked at the other statements. Kay had worked for Dale and Thurrock, Estate Agents, at their King's Highbury office. Her employer thought she was on holiday, colleagues ditto; neighbours thought she had 'gone away'. No one remembered seeing her for the best part of a week. Her car was parked in the same space outside the flats. No one seemed to have noticed that.

The photo of the girl was slightly blurry, as though it had been taken at an office party. Kay, pale-faced and serious, slightly apart, nursing an orange juice. Not the party type. Della took it from the file, building her own mental picture. A lonely girl, no friends, no family, no one to even notice when she went missing. The perfect victim.

Della opened Amanda's file next. Most of the

contents just went to confirm what she already knew. Amanda was reported missing on the 16th of March this year by Mary Spencer. There was an eighteen-hour delay between the last sighting and Mary's appearance at Western Road police station. Mary thought that Amanda had been staying with her boyfriend. Boyfriend had been questioned, but his story checked out: evening accounted for. Two-hour seminar, drink at the bar, balti and home with his mates.

The police had conducted extensive interviews across the university. Fellow students, academic staff, ground staff and porters, but no one had seen her after about 6.45 when she went to collect her bicycle from the porters' office. Appeals in the student paper, on the radio, posters around campus, had failed to bring any more information. It was a big site, with a population upwards of ten thousand. Even in a murder investigation, it was impossible to interview everyone, and this was not that, Della reminded herself, it was a missing person enquiry. The questioning was different. Do you know this girl? Did you see her on whatever date? Taking statements was an expensive, time-consuming business. Anyone not around on the day, anyone on holiday, or on a different shift, would be deemed as not having anything useful to contribute.

Della turned to the forensic. There was very little of this, apart from the bicycle. This had been found in the possession of a fifteen-year-old boy on a high-rise estate fifteen miles east of the university, right across the other side of the city. One of the local coppers had wanted to know how he'd got a ride like that. Found it in the river, he said, and the police believed him. Most of the prints on it were his, the rest unidentified. A fragment of the rear reflector light was discovered during the fingertip search of Wheeler's Lane. That fact had not appeared in the newspapers. Della noted it down.

There was less on the gifts and cards that Amanda had been receiving. The sender must have worn gloves and, contrary to advice from her housemates, Amanda had binned most of it. No reference to the Blues CD. If she had received it on the day she disappeared, it could have been included with her other stuff, no one realizing it had any significance.

Heather's file was about an inch thick. Della took the photograph out and put it with the others. She was dark haired, too, with large grey eyes, striking colour, the irises light towards the centre, with a dark corona. Della studied her face. She had been only fifteen when she disappeared, but she looked older; Annie Kelley had been wrong about that. The girl's features were clear and well defined, and went way beyond prettiness. She looked like someone. Della felt her heartbeat quicken. There was a resemblance in type between all of them, but . . . Della went to her briefcase, pulled out a file, and added another photograph. Blair Paige. Heather, the first girl to disappear, looked so like the star it was uncanny; only the eyes were different. Della leaned forward as another thought struck: maybe it was the other way round. Maybe Blair looked like Heather.

There was more about Heather than either of the others. Della read through the witness statements. Nearly four years ago, Heather had attended swimming practice at Stoke Park Leisure Centre, as she did every Thursday. She left, as normal, at 7.30, and had not been seen since. The date was February 16th.

All the staff on duty that night had been interviewed, along with team-mates, regular users and a water polo team. Water polo. Della circled that. Robert Travis had been coaching her. He had worked with Heather since the leisure centre had opened in September. He got on well with her. She was a very talented girl, popular, cool in competition, liked training, couldn't get enough. Fellow team members said she seemed happy that evening, no worries, nothing bothering her. None of them noticed anything out of the ordinary. Except one.

Della leaned, elbows on the desk, reading the statement of Tracey Rogers, the girl at the leisure centre. Tracey's opinion that Heather had lied, that she was meeting someone, was backed up by statements from her parents. They had not planned to pick their daughter up after swimming practice. Heather had made her own arrangements, which more than likely got her killed.

There were two witness statements, members of the public who had come forward, memories jogged by TV and newspaper appeals. A man out walking his dog, a woman getting off a bus. They had both seen a girl, fitting Heather's description, talking to a driver and then getting into a vehicle. That was where agreement ended. The night had been dark, and rainy. They could not even decide if the vehicle was a van or a car, let alone remember the registration number.

Della turned to the forensic reports. Heather's case had more than the other two put together. Her parents had retained all items sent and these had been subjected to extensive testing and follow-up investigations. The flowers had been ordered from a city centre florist's, paid for by Visa. There was some excitement about that, until they realized the card had been stolen. The actual owner was quickly eliminated.

Heather had also been sent a swimsuit – Della did not know about that – an expensive import. There was an asterisk, and someone had scribbled 'Fan?' in pencil. Della remembered the spectators' gallery. Heather was beginning to be known nationally and might have attracted something of a following, especially with her looks. The swimsuit looked promising. Shops and outlets were contacted. The brand was unusual, but not that unusual; that line of enquiry led nowhere.

Then there was the card. Della examined the photocopy. A store-bought valentine with none of the sinister customized touches of the one sent to Blair. The message, however, was the same: 'LOVE ME', in black capitals. Ink matched to Rotring.

She glanced through the other information. The CIO (Criminal Intelligence Officer) had looked at the cases, drawing connections. The girls had disappeared from a small area of the city, within a few miles of each other. This could mean the perpetrator was local, but he could also operate in other parts of the country, if nobody had picked up on it. The files were open, but each of the investigations had stalled as the lines of enquiry fizzled out.

All the girls had received unsolicited gifts and mail. They were young, of similar appearance; their disappearances followed a pattern. A year between Kay and Heather, almost a year to Amanda. And now? Della counted. If Blair was next, it was only four months. That didn't fit. Maybe she was wrong, maybe the cases were not related.

'Could be Rotring, could be anything'; her own words came back to her. Della looked at the forensic report, and then at the white envelope, hand-delivered, with her name on it. The printing was similar; to the naked eye the match was exact.

She shook the torn tarot card onto her desk, arranging and re-arranging the thumbnail-sized pieces, working on them like a puzzle, as she examined the photographs spread on her desk. All the women here were young, fit and attractive. Two of them, Blair and Heather, were beautiful.

Della stared at the faces, trying to think her way into the mind behind these disappearances. Cold and cunning, switching between godlike self-belief and bitter anger at a world which chose to ignore him. He was normal enough to function, not to attract attention, but his outward appearance disguised a personality defect as wide as a street. He had done this three times, at least, and got away with it. Blair's high profile made her a challenge, a suitable target. Blair's life was no different from the others, just more highly prized.

Her youth, her gender, her prominence would be a constant offence to him, like sand pouring into the raw wound of his self-esteem. He would not have missed the increased activity around her, the stakes getting higher. It wouldn't be long.

While she was thinking, her hand completed the tarot card jigsaw. Parts of the image were missing. The sword and the eyes had been carefully excised; the Queen of Swords had been rendered weaponless and blind.

Chapter 22

Della could not sleep. In the dark all she could see was the Tarot Queen, eyeless and impotent. The chilling symbolism was not lost on her, but how on earth had he found out? Who could have told him? Leonora? Hardly. Louise? Unlikely. That left Della herself. Who had she talked to about it? Not Wendy; she had hardly seen her partner since the case began. Who did that leave? Janine. The secretary had wheedled out every detail of the interview with Leonora, had been most upset that Louise had gone instead of her. And who would she have told? Mandy. And where would this conversation have taken place? That dippy New Age place. And what did they sell there, besides decaffeinated coffee? Tarot cards. Della lay in bed, hands behind her head. Oh, he was clever. She could almost see him laughing at her.

See him.

Della sat up, suddenly absolutely wide awake. He was clever, and a risk taker – 'Dead fit for an older guy' – a fragment of conversation she had overheard came back to her. Mandy had seen him. Maybe he was getting too clever by half.

Della snapped the light on and reached for the phone. The clock on the table told her it was four o'clock in the morning. There was no answer. Della replaced the receiver. Janine might not be there anyway. Her boyfriend, Ty, was a DJ; she was either still out at his club or had gone home with him. It would have to wait until the morning, but Della intended to be up and out bright and early.

Della was not the only one intending to make an early start. Blair had returned from an evening every bit as dreadful as Felicity had predicted. Stephen had been surly to the point of non-communication. Gina had gone so over the top it was like she was never going to come back; and then Bryn had arrived, just to top it all.

Blair had turned to Penny, Stephen's girlfriend, but there was no help there. She seemed a nice enough girl, but hardly said a word all evening, too overwhelmed by the high-octane atmosphere. She had regarded Blair with wide-eyed wonder. Not that Blair wasn't used to that. It was the normal reaction when people like Penny came face to face with a star. Blair had tried, had really tried hard, to be charming and act as normal and friendly as possible, using Louise as her model, but had been unable to thaw the other girl's starstruck awe.

Sometimes Blair felt as though she was living inside a glass castle, invisible walls all around her. That's why many of her Hollywood friends only hung out together and dated each other. Mixing with ordinary people was just too much hassle. The only people Blair knew who weren't like that, who did not treat her like some freaky monster, were Louise and Chris.

On her return, the evening got worse. Louise told her about Chris's visit, how upset he'd seemed when he heard their run was cancelled, how he had not even known that they planned on leaving. Blair could not believe that no one had told him. It looked bad, treating him like that. It would seem like typical rich-bitch movie star behaviour, and Blair did not want him thinking that about her. Felicity had absolutely no right cancelling things without Blair's say-so. The TV programme she was appearing on was a lunchtime thing; she did not have to be at the studio until ten. How long would a run take? What did Felicity think, that she was training for a marathon?

Anyway, she could do with the exercise, she reflected as she got out of bed. Her skin felt flushed; she had a headache. She had drunk more wine than usual; running would rid her body of the toxins and prepare her for the heat and lights in a stuffy TV studio. She brushed her hair to tie into a ponytail. It felt odd at the back, uneven. She tried to check but the mirror was at the wrong angle. How did that happen? One of the hairdressers at the studio could look at it. She needed to see Chris. She had something to tell him, and it had to be in person. Bryn had found a place. And they were leaving for it after her TV appearance, going to London straight from the studio.

It had been too late, last night, to catch him at the Health Club, but she had his home number. Before she went to bed, Blair had phoned his home and left a message.

She left quietly at 6.30. All around her the house was sleeping. Louise, in the next-door room, did not hear her friend's door closing. Her sleep contained no warning dreams and the step on the stairs was too light to rouse her.

Blair deactivated the alarm and let herself out into the day. It was beautiful, in a way that only an English summer morning can be. There were never days like this in LA. There the sun burned through the smog, shining white in a sky like a metal mirror. Here the sun was saffron yellow in a clear blue sky. Dew still sheened the grass, and white mist wisped up from the stream. Blair walked along gravel pathways and through pergolas heavy with the scent of roses, savouring the moment.

She had beauty, fame, every material thing anyone could ever want, but her life was constrained, confined. Guarded and watched all the time, she was rarely alone, and almost never had the chance to do what she liked. Times like this were few and far between.

She came out of the walk and looked to the trees at the end of the lawn. He would be there, waiting. Blair walked towards him, emerging from the long shadow cast by the house, leaving behind her long dragging footsteps. The dew was heavy there, soaking her training shoes, but the rising sun was strengthening, soon it would be full on this part of the grounds, drying the moisture, erasing her footprints.

When she got to the bridge, which took her across the stream and out of her own property, a figure stepped out of the sheltering trees, beckoning to her, grey tracksuit hood up. Chris liked to sweat so she thought little of it. Before she could get near enough to greet him, or speak to him, he set off. He kept in front, dictating the speed, choosing which paths to take. He turned to call her on; but every time she started to close, he speeded up, keeping a nagging gap between them.

After ten minutes Blair was beginning to feel the pace. It was fast, tough going, up and down hills, over rough ground.

She paused at a point where four paths crossed, to catch her breath and get her bearings. She knew these woods but they had gone zig-zagging back on themselves so often that she was feeling slightly disoriented. The leaves on the trees seemed to droop in the still early morning; some of them were already starting to turn although it was not long past mid-summer. She turned around and around, unsure of which way to go. There was no sign of him, no sound. Nothing stirred in the absolute silence. It was as though he was playing some kind of game with her. She looked left, the way they had come, thinking he might have doubled back, and then he suddenly appeared, off to the right, as if by magic.

Blair grinned with relief and, wiping away sweat with her bandanna, started up the long incline. The sun was behind him; she could see him outlined against it as he called her on. At the crest of the hill, under the trees, she could see his van. He must have driven along the track which bordered the eastern edge of the woodland. He did not usually drive, preferring to run through the health farm's landscaped grounds, but for once she was glad. Her legs felt like lead as she ran the last few sapping yards towards him. She didn't want to run all the way back.

Chapter 23

When Janine reached the office, Della was already there. Not that this was unusual – the detective was quite often in early, sometimes she didn't go home – but as soon as she came through the door, Janine knew there was something wrong. Della was sitting, white-faced and tense, behind Janine's desk, with Leonora Quinn's syndicated column spread out in front of her.

'Tell me, Janine,' the detective asked quietly, 'did you tell anyone about my visit to Leonora's?'

'I might have,' Janine answered, sensing the masked fury.

'Just answer. Yes, or no.'

'Well, yes. I might have mentioned it.'

'To whom?'

'To Mandy. But . . .'

'You know not to talk about cases, Janine. You have been told enough times.'

'Yes, but . . .'

'But nothing.' Della cut off the excuses. 'Either you did or didn't.'

'Well, I did, then.'

'When did this – conversation – take place?'

'The other lunchtime.'

'Where?'

'In the café. You know, the veggie place.'

'Did you know that this conversation was overheard?'

'No!' Janine shook her head, her beaded hair rattling denial.

'How do you account for the fact that I received this?'

Della threw the card on the table. She had pieced it together and stuck it onto board.

'I don't know, I . . .'

Janine looked at it and backed away, paling under her dark honey-coloured skin.

'OK, OK,' Della relented. 'Sit down and tell me what happened. Exact recall. And I want everything.'

Near to tears, Janine took the chair opposite Della.

'We was in there, Mandy and me, doing our stars and that, and I mentioned you'd been to see Leonora, because she's our favourite and I knew Mand'd be interested.'

'What about the tarot?'

'I might have said, I might have said, "Leonora agrees with me about Della".' Janine's voice became a whisper. 'I might have said something like that. There was a guy,' she added. 'Mandy said "Hi" to him. He might have heard us.'

'So where was this guy? Did you get a look at him?'

'No, not really. He was sitting kind of behind me. I didn't notice him until he said "Hi" to Mandy, and by then he was in the other part of the shop.'

'The tarot card-selling part?'

Janine nodded, ducking her head.

'You must have got some impression! Think about it!'

'Well, he was, I don't know, above medium height, dark haired, well built, strong legs. I noticed them walking past.'

'What was he wearing?'

'I don't know . . . jeans? Sweatshirt? I don't remember!'

'All right. Calm down.'

Janine was becoming distressed. Not that she didn't deserve it. She had been so stupid; Della had the right to put her through it, even sack her. But she looked so pathetic, all the sass bounced out of her, that Della took pity. 'We can always ask Mandy when she comes in.'

'No we can't.' Janine's voice was hardly audible. 'She's on holiday.'

'Since when?' Della stood up.

'Since yesterday. Apartment in Spain, but I ain't sure where.'

'Well, find out. Phone her mother. Find the tour company. Phone them,' Della rapped out. 'Now!'

Janine reached for the phone, but it rang before she could pick it up.

'FemTec Detective Agency, Janine speaking. How can I . . . Yes, she is. Hang on.' Janine put her hand over the mouthpiece. 'It's that woman who works for Blair. Felicity? She sounds very upset.'

*

By the time Della arrived at Blair's house, the guard on the gate had been replaced by a policeman. He waved her through when she explained her business. Squad cars lined the drive, some plain, some with stripes and light bars and the badge of the local constabulary. Dog handlers were unloading their charges. Police men and women in overalls were dispersing.

The door was open. Gina and Felicity were standing in the hall with a silver-haired guy in a Savile Row suit, who Della took to be Bryn. They were all talking at once to the same man. Della recognized him immediately and skirted round. She didn't wanted to be noticed yet. Just her luck for the officer in charge to be Jack Ryder.

'Now hang on a minute!' He put up his hands to stem the flow of words. 'If you'll *please* sit down, one of my officers will take your statements . . .'

Louise was standing on her own. Della went to join her.

'How long has Blair been gone?'

'I'm not exactly sure.' Louise looked at her watch. It was now nine thirty-five. 'No one noticed until around eight thirty when Felicity went to call her.' She turned a stricken face to the detective. 'Do you think . . .'

Louise's question was cut short by Detective Inspector Jack Ryder. As soon as he saw Della he left the group around him and came over to speak to her.

'Ah, if it isn't our very own private eye,' he

said. 'I wondered when you were going to turn up. I want a word.'

They went to Felicity's office. Ryder took up position by the desk, head back, arms folded. Della looked out at the activity going on outside the window and then turned to face him.

'So this is the case you were being so cagey about. You were supposed to be protecting Blair Paige, eh?' He rubbed at the shallow depression on the bridge of his nose as if sensitized by her stare. 'Well, you've done a great job so far, Della. I've got to hand it to you . . .'

Della studied the rug at her feet. If he was determined to have a go at her, it would be best to get it over.

'You, that boneheaded security mob, and the local plods. What a combination! Not only failing to secure her safety, almost guaranteeing her abduction . . .'

Della looked up as a sudden thought struck her.

'What are you doing here, anyway? This isn't your patch.'

'I'm here because I handled the Andrews kid enquiry.'

'The supermarket kidnapping?' Della shook her head. 'This isn't a kidnapping . . .'

'You might think that, Della, but you're not Chief Constable.'

'It's gone as high as that?'

Jack moved his forefinger, spiralling upwards.

'All the way. This girl is a celebrity, or hadn't you noticed?'

'But Jack, this is not a kidnapping. Treating it as one will put Blair's life in jeopardy. Look.' Della opened her briefcase. 'I can prove it. These cases are all related.' She spread the missing girls' files on the desk. 'Blair's next . . .'

'Oh, I see.' Jack looked down at them. 'This is why you were so thick with Helen. These are police files, Della. I can have you arrested for just looking at them.'

'Stop playing games, Jack, and listen to me.'

Della went over the connections between these cases, and explained how she thought they linked in with Blair.

Jack listened, but his expression remained sceptical.

'She's a celeb, Della.' He waved a hand at the cases in front of him. 'These are nobodies; the profiling, everything, is different. The smart money says this is a kidnap . . .'

'Yes,' Della was getting desperate now, 'but what if it isn't? He'll kill her, while you sit here twiddling your thumbs waiting for a call that never comes.'

To her horror, Della found her eyes were filling with tears. She moved away so he would not see if they spilled over.

'All right. All right.' He put a hand on her shoulder but she shrugged it off. 'I didn't mean to sound so hard. I'm sorry. It's just, given who she is, we'll get crucified if anything happens to her.'

Della blinked and sniffed. She had to get hold of herself here, pull herself together.

'What about the press?' she asked, trying to sound businesslike.

'There's a media blackout. There always is—'

'With a kidnap.' Della finished his sentence.

'Do you have anything, any other evidence, that you have not shown to us?' he asked, handing her a handkerchief.

Della shook her head, then she remembered Amanda's CD.

'Did anything else come this morning?' she asked.

'Yes, as it happens. A CD. It had a lock of hair in it. We reckon it's a softener for his ransom demand.'

'Was it a blues CD, by any chance?'

'Yes, it was.' He looked at her, curious. 'How do you know?'

'Amanda McCann received one, and I think she got it on the day she disappeared.'

'How can you be sure?'

'I can't be sure, I believe it, that's all. May I see?'

'On the desk. Help yourself. The hair is in a separate envelope.'

It looked like the same as the CD Amanda had received. Next to it, curled up in a plastic sleeve, was a hank of hair, thin and black, twisted in a figure of eight.

'No message?'

'That *is* the message.

'I suppose there'll be no doubt . . .'

'We've taken a sample from her hairbrush, but not in my mind. Where's the other disc? The one sent to McCann?'

'Back in the office.'

'I'll need that, and anything else. I'll send someone round. Meanwhile, we're setting up an incident room here, fixing up phone lines in case he calls.' He looked out of the window at the grounds. 'As well as searching the woods, and sending out descriptions to all the local forces.'

'Have you pulled anyone in?'

'Chris James, the guy she's supposed to have gone running with, and we're questioning the brother and his girlfriend. They are alibiing each other. Chris looks a better prospect – on paper . . . Trouble is,' Ryder rubbed his chin, 'he seems to have an alibi. The alarm was deactivated at 6.33; that's when we assume Blair left the house. We've interviewed three different people who swear he was standing in front of them at 6.30 doing early-bird aerobics in his Lycra pants. So,' he shrugged, 'we're holding him, for the moment, but any halfway decent lawyer will have him out of there in seconds flat. We reckon whoever it is was clocking the place disguised as him, and the security never cottoned on to it.'

'What about the dogs?' Della asked. The guards had been adamant: no unauthorized persons had accessed the premises. The dogs would have picked up an alien scent.

'Maybe he was wearing Chris's clothes, stole them out of his locker at that Greswoldes place.' Ryder shrugged again. 'We're looking into that. We're also running a check on all members and staff past and present. She was a regular; maybe he was, too. He'd have to scope her out before he made his move.'

There was a knock at the door. Ryder went to answer it.

'Excuse me, sir. One of the lads found this in the woods. Thought you ought to see it right away.'

The constable held a ladies' swimsuit in his hand. Size 10. Blair's size. Expensive California make. Green and orange. Della recognized it from the other day. It was Blair's swimsuit, and it had been cut to ribbons.

'Another one of his calling cards.' Jack turned his grim expression on to Della. 'There's nothing to stop you following your own line of investigation. Just as long as you return any material evidence to me as soon as possible.'

'OK. Can I take Louise?'

'Yeah. As long as she's made her statement.'

'Jack?' Della stopped on her way out. 'There's one thing you ought to know. It could be important. I think he's been hanging around my office. There's a girl, works in the office downstairs, she might be able to ID him.'

'Why didn't you say so before?'

'A lot's been happening.' She nodded towards the CD, the swimsuit. 'It slipped my mind. I'm telling you now, aren't I?'

'OK, OK, point taken. Where can I find her? I'll send someone . . .'

'There's a problem. She's in Spain, on holiday.'

Jack threw his pen down on the table. 'Oh, brilliant!'

'Janine, my secretary, is trying to find out where . . .'

'When she does, let me know. I'll send someone out there to get her if needs be. And Della?'

'Yes?' Della turned to face him.

'Good luck.'

Jack Ryder watched as she went. Part of him wished he could go with her, instead of sitting here waiting. She was a good detective. Thorough and intelligent, with the knack of getting people to talk, and the ability to make intuitive sense of what they told her. He valued her judgement. He glanced down at the files of the other missing girls. It would be good to have Della out there, following her hunches, just in case it wasn't a kidnapping, just in case they were wrong.

Louise was glad to be leaving, to be getting out of the hysteria building up inside the house. Having something to do kept her mind off Blair, what might have happened to her, be happening to her now. She was glad Della had asked her to help.

'The best thing to do is keep busy,' Della said, echoing her own thoughts. 'We'll check on Kay Walsh. I want to know more about her. See if we can pick up on something that might give us a clue as to who is doing this. She worked for an estate agent. King's Highbury. We'll start with her office.'

'Yes, Kay worked here for several years. Would you like to sit down?'

The manager was youngish, maybe thirty, but running to fat. It was going to be another hot day and he was already feeling it. Pink scalp showed through thinning fair hair and his face was sheened with sweat. He had taken off his jacket but circles marked his short-sleeved shirt under each arm.

'I can't help you a great deal, I'm afraid,' he said, rocking back in his executive chair. 'A bit of a loner, didn't chat a lot, just did her job. Didn't have much to do with anyone here. I don't know about her life outside work but I'd put her down for a loner there as well. You get to be a good judge of character in this job – you could try where she lived. Hang on a sec . . .' He reached into a filing cabinet and handed Della a brochure. The front showed low-rise flats, rendered in pastels. 'St Mary's Court. Corner of Church Street. Edgely address. Nice little properties, go like hot cakes. Kay had the show flat; part of her job was to show people round.'

Della frowned as she studied the brochure. Despite the idealized wishy-washy watercolour, something about the flats looked vaguely familiar.

'How long had she lived there?'

'Well, she joined us at about the time they were first put on the market, and moved straight in. That would be . . .' He worked it out on his fingers. 'About four years ago.'

'Would any of her stuff be at the flat now?'

'No. It was removed to storage. Nobody came to claim it.' He looked up, his hard-headed businessman pose slipping for a moment. His brown eyes were kind and compassionate. 'All alone she was, in this day and age, can you believe it?'

'Any of the neighbours remember her?'

'You could try, but I wouldn't hold your breath. High turnover, single-person occupancy. They all tend to be bit like Kay. Young professionals, keep themselves to themselves.'

Della looked down at her notebook. No friends. No family. Kay's life was lonely, lived in isolation amongst people who didn't want to know. For 'single-person occupancy' read 'bedsit'.

'Is there a site maintenance manager?'

He shook his head. 'Not now. Not for a couple of years. Once a property is fully onstream, there's less need for one.'

'You sacked him?'

'We prefer "rationalized".'

'Where are her belongings?'

'In one of our storage facilities.' He mentioned a site on the other side of the city.

'Did she . . .' Della started, choosing her words carefully. The right question might save a cross-town trip. 'Do you know if she ever received anything anonymous through the post?'

'Like what?'

His friendly openness suddenly closed down.

'Oh. Like valentine cards, flowers . . .'

'How do you know about that?'

Della folded her arms and waited for him to go on.

'Yes.' He looked embarrassed. 'She did, as it happens. She thought it was someone here, one of the lads, having a bit of a joke at her expense.'

'And was it?'

'Not as far as I know. She got pretty mad about it. Threatened to go to the police. Kay didn't have much of a sense of humour.'

'What happened? Did she report this harassment?'

'No. She disappeared before doing anything about it.'

'Did you mention it to the police?'

'Yes, but none of us had ever seen the stuff, and they found nothing. Could have been up here.' He tapped his temple. 'Who knows? Like I said, she was very lonely.'

'Just one more thing. Why didn't you report

her missing?' Della glanced around the busy office. 'You must have noticed.'

'It was Spring Bank Holiday; Kay was due a few days off. She'd been talking about going away. I assumed she had done.'

'It didn't occur to you to check?'

'Well, no. When the police walked in you could have knocked me down with a feather.'

Next on the list was BodySmiths Health and Fitness. It had been Dave Smith, the owner, who had reported Kay missing.

'Hi, the name's Dave, Dave Smith. How can I help you?'

Dave came out from behind BodySmiths Health and Fitness Club reception desk, hand outstretched to accept the card Della offered him. He was almost as broad as he was tall. The green BodySmiths T-shirt looked sprayed onto his wide chest and bunched shoulder muscles. His hair was cropped close and gelled so you could see the skull. He appeared hard, but when he smiled his blue eyes were mild, intelligent and friendly.

'Detective, eh? Well, well. Come with me. We'll find somewhere a bit more private.'

They followed him up a flight of stairs and along a corridor. His shorts clung tightly to powerful thighs, and he rolled from side to side, a bodybuilder's walk.

'Kay was one of our founder members.' He showed them into his office. 'She came every day, near enough, regular as clockwork. That's how I knew something was up. Never missed. She was dead keen. She was doing an instructor's certificate.'

'In what?'

'Aerobics.'

'When was that?'

'A couple of months before she went missing. I remember because we talked it over. She filled in sometimes, if we were short-staffed; she knew the routines off by heart. She wanted to know about becoming an instructor, so I told her about the course – recommended it to her.'

'Would she have been any good? I'd have thought you had to be pretty outgoing to do that kind of thing, and according to her boss, she was a bit of an introvert.'

'I know what you mean, but put her in a leotard, out on the dance floor, or up on the platform, and she was like a different person.' Muscles rippled as he shrugged his huge shoulders. 'She had a superb body and liked to show it off. The only doubt I had was about her knee.'

'Her knee?'

'She'd torn the ligaments about a year before. She'd undergone a course of treatment, up at the hospital, but it was still playing up.'

'I see . . . You said she was doing a course. Which college?'

'King's Highbury. Leisure and Recreation Department.'

'A couple more things . . .'

Louise only half-listened as Della ran through her questions. Instead she watched Dave Smith. Something about him, his stance and gait, the way he sat, reminded her of someone.

'That's it.' Della stood up. 'Thanks, Mr Smith. You've been very helpful. If there's anything else, I'll be in touch.'

'Hey, call me Dave.' Della's hand disappeared in his grasp but his grip was gentle. 'Anything I can do, you know? Take one of these.' He swept a leaflet off the desk and presented it to her. 'It's got our number, you're welcome to a complimentary class.' He looked her up and down and grinned. 'I don't know where you go, but you obviously keep in shape. Why not try us?'

Della smiled back. 'I haven't had much time lately but, yes,' she glanced down at the list of classes, 'maybe I will.'

'You do that,' he replied, his grin spreading wider as he shepherded them towards the door. 'What about you?'

With a shock, Louise realized he was talking to her.

'Oh, er . . .'

Della laughed. 'I'll bring her, too.'

'You haven't said much.' He winked at Della. 'Left it all up to your boss. Don't you have any questions?'

'Well, yes, as a matter of fact. Do you know Chris James?'

His grin faded. He looked as though the newel post had spoken.

'Yes, I know him. We used to train together.'

He folded his arms. Biceps bulged against equally massive pectoral muscles.

'Here?'

'No, love.' He shook his head, smiling to himself at the thought of it. 'This isn't his kind of place. We used to work out at Murphy's. I can tell you're ex-force,' he glanced at Della, 'you ought to know it.'

Della nodded. She knew it all right. Murphy's Gym was well known in the city, pre-dating the emergence of these health and fitness clubs by a good couple of decades. It was a boxers' gym, popular with bodybuilders and weightlifters, awash with steroids. It was situated not far from the old Jubilee baths where they were yesterday. The gym operated above a seedy row of pawn shops and Balti houses. Lots of guys from the police trained there. Partly, Della suspected, because it was strictly Men Only. There wasn't a notice to that effect on the door, of course – that would be against the law – but it was understood that women were not welcome and never would be. Not that any woman in her right mind would want to go there. You could smell the sweat out on the street, mingled with tandoori.

'I haven't been up there for a while,' he added. 'Too busy with this place. What's he doing now?'

'He's at The Greswoldes.'

He laughed, short and sharp. 'Well, stone me.

I'd never have thought that, never in a month of Sundays.'

'Why not?' Louise asked.

'It's not his kind of place. Last time I talked to him he was serious about wanting to work with sportsmen. Boxers, mainly. He could be a really great trainer. He's got it up here.' He tapped his forehead. 'Knows how to get people to focus, concentrate. I didn't think he'd end up somewhere like that. I wonder what made him change his mind?'

'Yeah, well, there you go,' Della replied absently. 'We'd better be off. Thanks for your help.'

Kay Walsh was suddenly back in the forefront of her mind. Something had been niggling, something about that block of flats. Suddenly it dropped into place.

'That was a good question about Chris,' Della said, picking up the carphone. 'We'll make a detective out of you yet. Can you get that estate agent's brochure for me? And the *A to Z*.'

Louise rummaged through the stuff on the back seat.

Della checked out her hunch. 'I knew it!'

'Knew what?'

'This block of flats.' Della indicated the picture. 'Steven's girlfriend's place is right opposite . . . Oh, hello, is that King's Highbury College?' She was speaking into the phone now. 'I'd like to talk to someone in the Leisure and Recreation Department . . .'

Della pretended to be a prospective employer in order to establish that Christopher James had studied on a four-year course for a degree in Leisure Management, which he had just completed. She also discovered that the course was split between the college and Mercia University and included a third year semester in the States, running from September to April. Chris's choice of college was UCLA, University of California, Los Angeles.

'What was that all about?' Louise asked, when she completed the call.

Della drew three circles on a page in her notepad. Inside each she wrote the different girls' initials – HG, FW, AMcC. Then she drew another circle with CJ in the middle. His circle bit into each of the others.

'He knew Heather.' She wrote 'swimming' in her shared segment. 'He studied at the same college as Kay. The course took him to the university and Amanda.' She wrote 'Coll' and 'Univ' in their segments. 'He also spent time in the States.' She added a circle with Blair's name in it.

Louise frowned. 'Wouldn't the police have picked up on that?'

'Not necessarily. All we've established is a connection. Tell me, Louise, how many people know you?'

'Not that many.'

'How about all the people in your school?'

'Well, yes, but . . .'

'People at the bus stop. In shops. In clubs, bars, discos, the library, any place you regularly go to.'

'But they don't *know* me.'

'They know you exist. Hundreds of people "know" us like this. If you take someone like Blair it's millions. What if one of them, just one, is watching you, taking notice for a special purpose? You aren't going to know, unless they want you to, or until it's too late. That's how stalkers operate. Close in, but not close enough to be noticed. The police can't interview every single acquaintance, even in a murder inquiry, let alone the guy who gets on the bus the stop before yours most days, or stands three back from you in the dinner queue, and sits where he can watch you but you can't see him. See what I mean?'

'Mmm . . . But I can't see how the police could have missed this. It seems pretty conclusive.'

'OK. We'll try something else.'

Della kept the four girls the same, but put another circle in the middle, this time with the initials SF in the middle.

'Stephen!'

'Yes. Just watch. HG – water polo. KW – sports injury and flat. AMcC – University and girlfriend. BP – brother. And how about this?' She scribbled out SF and wrote in the segments: 'HG – swimming, Jubilee baths. KW – estate agents, flat-hunting. AMcC – university course.'

'Who's that?' Louise asked.

'Me.'

Louise did not reply. She could see the point Della was trying to make, but it made the person behind it all seem more shadowy than ever.

'Don't worry. Other stuff will mesh in and we'll find her. There's still the CDs; we haven't had a major think about them yet.'

'I thought you'd given it to Jack?'

'Not before Janine went to the record store. We're going back to the office.'

Chapter 24

'Any luck?' Della asked as she came through the door.

'Yeah.' Janine looked up from her console. 'Mandy's mum gave me the resort, flight number, and the name of the tour company. I've faxed 'em to Ryder. Oh, and a Mary Spencer phoned.'

'What did she want?'

'Said to tell you that the name of the group who played Amanda's tune was White Trash.'

White Trash? Louise had never heard of them.

'Local blues band, big in the sixties,' Janine explained, 'I checked with Ty.'

'Get on to the radio stations, find out which one sent out the dedication and which track.' Della stood still for a moment, excitement tingling through her. The clue they needed: this could be it. 'Bring Janine's portable stereo,' she said to Louise. 'We're going to listen to the blues.'

Louise followed Della into her office.

'This CD is a blues compilation recorded by original artists. Sent to Blair and Amanda, both young girls. This isn't their kind of music. Why would anyone send them that?'

'There must be something on it,' Louise replied. 'Something significant, like a title, or lyrics.'

She frowned, unable to take it further. Significant in what way? To whom? And which one? Blues numbers were short; the CD carried twenty tracks, all by different artists.

'OK.' Della wrote the tracks on a whiteboard. 'We'll concentrate on love songs, eliminating those that don't profile.' She wrote *Obsession, Anger, Vengeance, Jealousy.* 'We'll work separately, and see if we agree.'

Louise listened carefully at first, then her attention began to wander. She looked at the list on the board; they all seemed to be about those kinds of things, they all sounded the same to her. Then one song caught her, and held her.

'Wait,' she said, 'play that one again.'

Della skipped back.

An old man's voice, thin and high, wailing out a young man's frustration and misery, slide guitars slipping over the ragged emotions, harmonicas howling fury, a saxophone held at the pitch of a young girl screaming.

Della reached for her pen. 'This could be it.' She handed Louise the paper. 'Read the words.'

Killing Time Blues
Been sitting here thinking what you done to me
Just killing time thinking what you done to me
It's a pure crime, baby, and that ain't no lie
Things you do, make a strong man cry
You hurt me so bad, baby, give me the killing time blues

All night thinking, waiting by the phone
You ain't called, momma, lef' me all alone
Coming up 'round about midnight I go out to roam

You been a bad girl, baby, gonna bring you home
Makes me so sad, baby, to have the killing time blues

Watch the clock ticking, tick your life away
Hour is coming when you're gonna pay
Yeah that hour is coming, time for you to pay
I ain't joking, baby, just you wait and see
Gonna do everything that you done to me
Ain't got nothing to lose, with these killing time blues

Been a bad time, baby, but it's ending soon
Right around midnight, you're gonna sing my tune
In that hour 'bout midnight, you're gonna get the news
You been a bad girl, momma, time to pay your dues
You been so bad, baby, got those killing time blues.

'The White Trash track was called "Killing Time".' Janine came in from the outer office. 'City FM. They do a regular "Our Tune", call it "Late Night Love Spot". Had a request for it to go out again this week. Tonight to be exact.'

Louise and Della stared at her.

'You aren't serious?'

'The bloke just told me. The dedication is to Isabel Franklin.' Louise felt cold spread through her; that was Blair's real name . . . 'But they aren't doing it.'

'Why not?'

'Because they played the same song three months ago, for Amanda; even they think that's iffy. Is that what you've just been playing?'

'Yes. The blues original. Listen.'

Della played the song again and Janine concentrated on the lyrics, caught in the powerful, compelling blues rhythm. There was a kind of message there, under the words, and it was sinister, chilling. Hopeless love, plaintive longing, curdling into bleak, bitter anger and revenge.

'It's not exactly a love song,' she commented.

'Maybe not. But that's where it started.' Della paced the room. 'The things he sends, valentine cards, flowers, they are love tokens. What if that first time they were genuine?'

'You mean Heather Griffiths?'

'Yes! What if they were sent by a secret lover, whose identity was known to her but not to anybody else? Then something happens. Maybe she rejects him, gets cold feet, wants out. Wires cross, a new kind of behaviour starts in someone whose wiring is badly defective. Gifts, originally sent in love, become part of a bizarre ritual, leading up to some kind of final act . . .'

'That the song kind of describes and anticipates at the same time,' Louise said, picking up her line of thought.

'Exactly. In some way Heather's the key. All we've got to do is figure out how. Who was she going to meet?'

'All the girls look like each other,' Louise said. 'Especially if you look at their pictures all together.'

'But who do they look like? Blair or Heather? Janine – get on to Jack Ryder. He needs to know about this. We need to get that song back on the playlist.'

*

'This has to do with place,' Della said as she wove through the lines of traffic, changing lanes, and back through the ring roads and merging motorway interchanges which cradled the city. 'This is his patch, his territory. I don't think he operates outside it. He stays put and waits, like a spider.'

'But what about Blair?' Louise asked as the densely packed streets relaxed into suburban roads. 'How could he know she would wander into his web?'

'I have no idea. But in some way he must have. I also think that's why he's struck now. He knows that soon she'll be out of his reach. It's got to be someone close to her.'

'Like Chris James?'

Della nodded.

'He could have been in America, last year, when Kay disappeared.'

'He wasn't. The US semester had finished by then. Could be him. Could be Stephen.'

'Stephen?' Louise repeated. She did not want to think it was Blair's brother. 'Why him? I thought he'd been ruled out.'

'Why? Because of his girlfriend?' Della shook her head. 'Water polo players were using that new leisure centre pool at the time Heather disappeared. Stephen is a water polo player.'

'So are lots of people!' Louise objected. 'You don't know it was his team.'

'Yes, I do. The university pool was out of commission that term. He lived opposite Kay Walsh;

plus he might have seen her at the clinic – given his interest in sports injuries.'

'What about Amanda McCann?'

'She and his girlfriend were doing the same courses.'

Louise frowned. She didn't believe it was Stephen, but she could see how easy it was to build up the case against him.

'What about motive?' she asked. 'Blair's his sister!'

'Exactly. He's fixated on her. Full of conflicting feelings; loves her one minute, hates her the next. He blames her for the family break-up, his exile to boarding school. But he also wants to protect her, look after her, play big brother.' Della paused, deciding whether to say the next thing; in the end she did: 'Maybe he even fancies her. Given their long separation – she leaves as a child, comes back as a woman. If you add that she's a star, and the kind of star she is . . .'

Louise stared at her, ready to deny even the possibility. Then she remembered Stephen's reaction to the film, the way he'd kissed Blair in the hall.

'What about his girlfriend?' she said at last. 'She was the one who caused all the trouble.'

'You can look at that two ways. Either she acted out of jealousy, provoked by his obsession with Blair, or . . .'

'Or what?'

'Or they're in it together.'

'They can't be . . . I mean, she's a woman . . .'

'So? It doesn't happen often, but it can be a couple working together, abducting girls, usually at the instigation of the male partner; the woman acts as a decoy. I'm not saying that's the case here, but it's possible; we have to consider all angles. You can't let personal feelings get in the way.'

'I suppose so,' Louise muttered, suddenly uncertain.

'On the other hand,' Della said, looking right as she reached the roundabout, 'it could be Chris. There's plenty of evidence to link him with each girl, particularly Heather. But none of this is proof. Connection on its own is not enough.'

'So what are you going to do?'

'Keep searching, keep looking.' Della took the second turning, the one for Ashbury village. 'I'm going back to the very first incident, the flowers that freaked out Leonora.'

'I thought you'd checked on that before?'

'I might have missed something,' Della shrugged, 'something new might turn up. We need some luck on this case. What's the time?'

'Near on six o'clock.'

'Six hours till midnight,' Della said. 'That's how long we've got to find her.'

Della played the blues track in the car, until the snarling guitars seemed to tear Louise's brain, making her head ache, and she had to ask for it to be turned off. The feeling that they were getting somewhere was haemorrhaging into terror for Blair and what might be happening to her.

Della parked in Ashbury's multi-storey. Covered walkways led to the shopping centre. All the shops were shutting.

'I'll meet you back at the car,' Della said, breaking into a run. 'I want to catch the florist's before it closes.'

Louise wandered along at her own pace. She rounded the corner of the car park and crashed into someone big and hard.

'Hey, steady on.' Hands on her shoulders caught and held her. 'Are you OK?' Recognition replaced polite enquiry as the voice said, 'Louise! Where are you off to?'

The collision left her dazed but she knew, straight away, that she had charged into the arms of Chris James.

'I'm, er, trying to get to the shops.'

'They're closing.'

'I know.'

'You're all shaken up.' He looked down at her, brown eyes contrite. 'I'm really sorry . . .'

'It's my own fault. I wasn't looking where I was going . . .'

'Do you want to sit down? Or shall I run you home?'

'No, it's OK. I'll be fine. Really . . .'

'Well, you don't look OK. Come on. I've got the van. I'll give you a lift.'

'Really – there's no need . . .'

But before she could protest further, or explain

about Della, he had taken her arm and was leading her back towards the car park entrance.

'I want to talk to you,' he said. 'Blair's gone missing and the police think I did it.'

'I'm sure they don't . . .'

'Yes, they do.' His grip on her arm tightened. 'They've been questioning me nearly all day.' He stopped as they entered the bottom level, holding the door for her to go through. Inside the air was thick with fumes but most of the vehicles had departed. Della's car was by the entrance ramp. His van stood alone right over in the far corner. 'Why would the police think I had anything to do with it?'

'I – I don't know.'

'I think you do.' He was standing behind her. 'There's something you ought to know. There's something I want to tell you. But first,' he gripped her shoulders, 'you're all tense, you ought to learn to relax a bit . . .'

She stared at the concrete floor, ridged and discoloured, patched with oil, as his fingers moved from her clavicles to slide across the large muscles either side and circle her neck. Her blood pulsed against fingertips pressing into the flesh below the angle of her jaw as strong thumbs explored up under her hair to connect with the base of her skull.

'Relax, that's it,' he whispered, his voice as soft as fur in her ear. 'I'm not going to hurt you. Trust me and it won't hurt a bit.'

*

Outside the florist's shop, a woman was collecting up buckets of flowers. The shop exhaled a complex scent, distilled by the heat of the day, conflicting perfumes edged with decay.

'Can I help you?' the woman asked. 'Only we're closing.'

'I don't want flowers,' Della said. 'Just information. I came earlier in the week, but you weren't here. I spoke to your partner. Did you deliver to Portland House?'

'Yes.' The woman recognized the name. 'White and red roses, arranged them myself.'

'Was there a card with them?'

'Yeah. Wrote that and all, said: "Welcome Back." It was raining that morning.' She shook her head. 'Hard to believe, weather like this. The gates were stuck half open. I looked but couldn't see any guard chap. I was that annoyed. July is a busy time, I was late and the van was packed. I was just about to give up and leave them by the gate, when this chap appeared from inside the grounds. He offered to take them. I reckoned he must live there, or work there, so I handed them over.'

'Do you remember what he was wearing?'

'Tracksuit. Greswoldes logo.'

'How do you know that?'

'Deliver there, don't I?'

'Anything else? What he looked like? Height? Build?'

The woman shook her head. 'He had his top up and it was raining. Tell you what, though. I saw a chap, a minute ago, looked just like him . . .'

'Where!'

'Going towards the multi-storey car park.'

'Are you OK?' Della came dashing back to find Louise standing by the car. 'Was Chris here?'

'Yes.'

'He didn't . . .'

'Of course not, Della,' Louise answered. She rolled her head. All the tension was gone. 'I'm perfectly all right.'

She had been scared, badly scared, but all he had done was massage her neck and shoulders.

'What did he want?'

'To talk about Blair.'

'What did he say?'

'He said he loves her. He said he knows it's hopeless, given who she is, but he could never do anything to harm her. He'd rather die himself than do that.'

'Mmm, maybe,' Della said, but she still did not trust him.

The smell outside the florist's shop had reminded her of Leonora. In her mind, she heard again the low musical voice saying: ' . . . I felt the touch, the merest brush, of a hand capable of the most terrible cruelty.'

Chapter 25

'My money's still on James. He ties in with all of them and he profiles perfectly.' Della counted the points off: 'Fractured family history, mother absent, difficult relationship with a domineering father, possibly abusive. Feelings of failure, inadequacy . . .'

Ryder was sitting on the edge of Felicity's desk, shaking his head. The strain of the day was beginning to show, tie askew, shirt wrinkled and clinging to his chest. Dark hair fell over his eyes and five o'clock shadow emphasized his natural pallor. Tension lines were carved at the sides of his mouth, etched round his narrow blue eyes.

Felicity's office had been transformed into an incident room. A whiteboard, covered in scrawls, stood against one wall. Extra phone lines had been patched in but the tape recorders had not turned, the tracking systems had not been used, there had been no communication. Uniformed officers sat at computer consoles. Girls' faces looked down from a pinboard, not just Blair, the other three were up there as well.

'I know how you feel, Della.' Jack pinched the bridge of his nose. 'But his alibi is rock solid. We can't touch him.'

'He must have taken her, stashed her somewhere . . .'

Ryder shook his head again. 'Impossible. We've got his every movement accounted for.'

Della frowned. She didn't believe that. He was clever. Very clever. He must have managed it somehow.

'So what are you going to do?'

'What we've been doing all day. Keep on searching. Sit here and wait.'

'Christ, Jack!' Della looked at her watch. It was twenty past eight. 'You haven't got time for that. Didn't you listen to that song? We've got until midnight.'

'Ah, the song.' He pushed a hand through his hair. 'The powers that be don't agree with you on that one.'

'What do they think? That it's got nothing to do with it?'

'No. They don't think that. The song is back on the playlist. They're very grateful to you for spotting it, but they think it's a public signal, put there to mark the beginning of his ransom demands.'

'This is not about money.' Della snorted with contempt. 'They're signing her death warrant. No one will ever see her again.' Della nodded towards the photographs on the board. 'She's going to end up like them.'

'I tend to agree with you.' Ryder stared at the smiling faces. 'I put those up as a reminder, and I've got people combing through the cases, but . . .' He shrugged, a gesture of hopelessness.

'Where's James now?'

'He's at Murphy's Gym.' Ryder consulted a clipboard. 'He's given me a list of his intended movements. He's been very cooperative. He's involved in some project, training kids from the neighbourhood to beat each other up in a controlled environment, you know the kind of thing. Don't worry. I've got a couple of lads there keeping an eye on him, because, guess what?' He gave a mirthless laugh. 'It's a community policing initiative.' He got off the table. 'Better crack on. By the way, Della. I've been told to tell you. Thanks for what you've done so far, but do any more and they'll pull your licence.'

Della parked on the Western Road, nearly opposite Murphy's Gym. The street was a different place after dark. Ragga pounded from a record shop sound system and the drinkers from the pub on the corner were outside in the warm summer night, sitting on the steps or leaning against walls, pints propped on window ledges. People strolled past eating takeaways from the chip shops and kebab places, or peered at the menus outside the tandoori restaurants and Balti houses.

Louise sipped her coffee and studied the street life while Della sat next to her, tearing chunks out of her plastic cup, staring across to the open stairway where the neon sign, *Mur hy's G m*, stuttered on and off. She was waiting for Chris James. What she would do when he came out,

Louise didn't like to ask. She was here on sufferance.

She had not wanted to stay at the house, just waiting around, watching the police activity, comforting a tearful Felicity. Gina had been put to bed, sedated. Louise had pleaded with Della to let her come. Jack Ryder had said it would be OK, the fewer people under his feet the better and, after all, they were only going back to Della's office. That was not what Della had in mind but, rather than let him know that, she had to agree to take the girl. She was going to drop her off home, but time was getting tight. In the end Della had allowed her along on the strict understanding that Louise did as she was told.

So this was surveillance. Louise finished her coffee, boredom beginning to smother the first rush of nervous anticipation. It didn't seem to affect Della. She just sat there, motionless. Her profile, lit by the street lights, seemed carved out of stone.

'How come you're so sure it's him?' Louise asked. 'I mean, why would he need to? He's attractive, good looking – and he's really nice.'

'So was Ted Bundy,' Della replied without turning round.

'Who was Ted Bundy?'

'An American law student. Young, well spoken, clean cut, handsome. He went to the electric chair for twenty killings and he was probably responsible for the deaths of twice as many women.'

'But this is different. Chris says he loves Blair!'

Della gave a humourless grin. 'All the more reason.'

'But how could he have done it? He's got an alibi.'

'I don't know how. That's what I'm trying to figure out. He's got her stashed somewhere, must have. Now he's biding his time, waiting.'

'Waiting for what?'

'Waiting for midnight.'

He'd seen Della's car soon after she pulled up. She had not bothered to hide her presence, but he wasn't hiding, either. He did not know why she was there, and cared less. Two tracksuited policemen had been with him all evening. The officers were mates of his, members of the gym. They were in the back room now playing pool, keeping less than watch, but they trusted him and did not see the need to cuff or lean on him. They had an understanding.

Ryder was due back to take another crack at him, but the policeman was taking his time, he was that kind of guy. He'd been that kind of boxer. Feinting, weaving, jabbing teasing little blows until – *pow!* He'd hit when you least expected. He interviewed like that, too. Chris was steeling himself for another round of questioning about Blair, and it could take all night, never mind his alibi. But it was not Blair Paige on his mind as he sipped from a can and gazed out of the window at Della's car. He was thinking about Heather Griffiths.

Heather had been going to see him that night, the night she disappeared. He was the one she was supposed to meet. She had come to him, asking to see him, saying she had something very important to tell him, something she could not speak about to anybody else. He knew exactly what she had to say, but he agreed to meet her anyway. He had never told the police that. He had kept it to himself. Never told a soul. Why not?

The metal crumpled, tearing like paper as he twisted the can between his hands. Was it possible? He'd heard about it, read about it, seen it on TV documentaries. What did they call it? Repressed memory. Bad memories were taken out and replaced. Your past became edited, erased, re-recorded on to a different tape. Could he be suffering from that?

He was doing it again. Even as the idea was forming, another part of his mind was ready to refashion it. He recognized the process for what it was. Evasion. Denial. Every thought, every remembered incident, carefully cut and tailored into something more acceptable. What if the memory was true? What if he knew? Had always known. Could he, could anybody, be that damaged?

You could see a lot from up here. He saw the van turn in further up the street. He looked down for Della and she was gone. It was time. It was time now. He turned away from the window. Time to get it sorted.

'Where are you going?'

'I'm going to check around.' Della reached into the back. 'I want to have a look at his van.'

'Won't the police have done that?'

'Yes. This morning. He's been driving around since then. He might have dumped her, then gone and got her. She might be in it now. Stay in the car. Lock all the doors. Don't get out for any reason at all. I'll be back soon.'

'But what if you aren't?'

'Call me on the carphone. Just stay put. I won't be long, I promise.'

'Della! *Della!*' Louise yelled after her, but the detective had gone. 11.35. 11.36. Little red figures on the dashboard clock. Louise locked the doors and slid down, hoping none of the gangs of youths reeling past would notice her.

'Hey! Baabee! You wanna come with us?'

Louise looked up to see a grinning boy in a turned-around baseball cap. He banged on the window, palms flat, to get her attention.

'This your car? Nice car.'

'What you doing sitting there all by yourself?'

There was another face on the driver's side. One of them had surfed on to the bonnet and lay, spreadeagled, waving at her through the windscreen. She was surrounded. They were high spirited rather than threatening, stoned or drunk, but there were about five or six of them and their festive mood could turn in an instant to ugly confrontation. Louise breathed faster, fear breaking out all over her, and sat tight, trying to ignore them, as they circled the car bombarding her with a fusillade of invitations, comments and questions.

'You got a boyfriend? What's he doing leaving you?'

'C'mon baby, come with us!'

'We're going to a club.'

'You'll have a good time. Honest . . .'

Louise looked round for help. No one, none of the passers-by, seemed the slightest bit interested. Whatever was about to happen, Louise couldn't handle it. She reached for the carphone.

'I'll have that. Nice piece.'

The window caved in. Sugar-crystal nuggets of shatterproof glass scattered all over her as a hand reached in.

The boy with the phone grinned and lifted it to his head in salute, and then they fled up the street, dissolving into the crowd, disappearing as suddenly as they had come, like a flock of starlings.

Louise left the car. She couldn't sit there with a shattered window and glass all over her. She reached down through the empty space into the map pocket for a torch. She didn't really need it but the heavy weight made her feel safe. She was going to find Della.

The detective had crossed the road to Murphy's

Gym. Louise was intent on following when she heard a cry from behind her.

'There she is!'

'Hey, baby. You changed your mind!'

It was those boys again. They had appeared, as if from nowhere, and had arranged themselves on corners, both sides of the street, so any way she went they were bound to catch her.

Louise ran back along the main road and ducked down a side street. There were plenty of people around, so she didn't feel that scared. She intended to cut along one of the short connecting roads, and get back to the main thoroughfare further up, but in the milling crowds and unfamiliar territory she quickly became disoriented. The cries behind her faded into general street sound; she'd lost the boys but, as she stopped to get her breath, she realized she'd lost herself as well.

She looked around. At first nothing struck her as familiar and all she could feel was fear mounting inside her. On her own, in a quiet side street, in this part of town, was not a safe place to be; and then she saw Benfield Forging. She was by the side of the old swimming pool. It was only twenty yards or so to the main road. She'd been here yesterday with Della.

She flashed her torch at a set of rusty gates. UNSAFE BUILDING DO NOT ENTER. Past the notice, the beam glinted on glass. There was a van parked up from the entrance, behind a bush. It looked similar in size and model to the one she'd seen in the multi-storey car park. The one driven by Chris James.

Louise stood for a moment, weighing the options. She could go and find Della, but that would take time. A quick look first would not hurt. She pushed the gate. The chains were not padlocked; there was just enough space to squeeze through.

When she got near, she began to doubt it was the same van. It looked similar but the back window was blocked up. A voice, hammering in her head, was telling her to go, find Della, get out of here, when she saw a scrap of yellow bandanna, under the rear wheel. Louise knelt down. It was like the one Blair wore round her neck when she went running.

Louise stood, her legs trembling so much they could hardly hold her. By the time she found someone, and explained, and waited for them to believe her, it would be too late. The clock on the university tower had already struck the quarter hour. She checked her watch. It was ten minutes to midnight.

Chapter 26

Louise flashed her torch over the rear of the building. The old swimming pool was the perfect place to hide someone: boarded up, covered with notices saying it was an unsafe structure. So what if she screamed? No one would hear in the general street din. In this kind of neighbourhood screams were commonplace; no one would take any notice. The main road carried life to and from the city; either side the streets were dead, deserted. So near, yet so far from any kind of help. Police sirens sounded all times of the night and day but always going to somewhere else. You could hold someone here for days, weeks; but Louise knew he was not working to that timescale.

A piece of rotten plywood had been prised away from one of the windows. Underneath the glass was smashed. Louise pushed the flap of splintering wood and climbed into an atmosphere thick with the smell of mould and rot, laced with the stench of chlorine.

A corridor stretched into darkness so absolute it seemed to eat torchlight. A series of heavy doors led off. Louise opened them one after another. Rusting hinges squealed back and deep enamel baths yawned like coffins in the narrow, shadowy cobwebbed rooms. The torch gleamed on dirty white enamel, stained and pitted like ancient kidney dishes, old-fashioned mortuaries. Once or twice the red eyes of rats shone back. Louise thought of Della's story about the tramp, and kept expecting to see his dead face, rotting and stiff, leering up at her, but she made herself check each cubicle before pushing the chrome-barred door which led into the entrance hall.

She paused, playing her torch over old notices curling on the walls. All dated four years ago. The dust of years furred the mahogany counter, but no footmarks walked across the drifting dirt on the black and white tiled floor, or smeared the piled pigeon droppings.

She picked her way carefully across the mess and entered the door to the right. FEMALE CHANGING. Pegs and benches stood in rows. The wire baskets, which used to hold clothes, heaped in piles. Louise skirted them and went on, silent as a ghost, past the changing cubicles, through the empty shower stalls that would take her into the swimming pool proper.

The sound froze her to the wall. Hairs stirred on the back of her neck, her ears seemed to move on her head. Distant but clear, someone was talking. Not outside. Here. Inside the building. The voice was brash, light hearted, inconsequential. Somewhere a radio was playing. It was so ordinary, so everyday, that for a moment she was at a loss to know what it was.

Her hand shook, making the light wave around. Louise switched her torch off and slipped round the footbath and onto the poolside tiles.

This area had a glass roof. Whole sections had fallen in, opening it up still further. There was light enough from the outside to see where the huge panes now lay smashed at the bottom of the drained pool, glittering like black ice, among a tangled mess of bent and twisted metal.

The radio acted as a directional beacon. Louise looked towards the diving boards at the deep end. The sound seemed to be coming from behind and above them.

Stairs led to the spectator gallery. The rail was shaky, flaking, but her feet made no sound on the wrought iron as she went up and along the aerial walkway. The radio was getting louder. She was near enough now to hear the words the DJ was saying, to hear the powerful blues guitar, the driving opening bars:

> 'OK out there – you know who you are. You've been blitzing us with messages but you can chill now, we're going to play your song. And this is for [*pause while he read the name*] Isabel Franklin! Pretty name for a pretty girl, eh, Isabel? Listen up, girl, this is for you, from someone who thinks you are very, very special. You be good to him now! Here it is, near to midnight as we can get it, local lads, White Trash with those old Killin' Time Blues!'

. . . been sittin' here thinking what you done to me . . . Louise edged along the walkway towards the sound ... ***Pure crime, baby, that ain't no lie***... She could see Blair now, half lying, half sitting, on some kind of platform, trussed up in a sleeping bag, orange rope looped and tightened round and round. She was alive. The hood quivered as she breathed in and out ... ***Comin' up round midnight, I go out to roam, been a bad girl, baby, gonna bring you home***... The voice sang on, rough and nasal, a white boy singing a black man's music, intoning the words over the heavy drumming and guitars screaming ... ***Watch the clock ticking, tick your life away***... He must be here, somewhere; Louise risked another move forward ... ***hour is coming, time for you to pay***... the voice went on, hard and strong. If she could just get to Blair ...

A dark figure stepped out of the shadows, and ripped the hood from Blair's head.

... ***you been a bad girl, momma***... Blair's eyes opened wide, huge in her chalk-white face, and as black as the insulation tape plastered over her mouth ... ***time to pay your dues***... A blade flashed in his hand. Blair became more and more agitated, throwing her head from side to side, muffled sounds coming from her mouth, despite the gag, as a human voice, thin and high, crooned to the radio ... ***ain't got nothin' to lose, got those killin' time blues***...

Some slight sound must have alerted him to another presence. He turned his head halfway, his face hidden by the hooded top he was wearing, his body crouched and still, like an animal disturbed from a kill. Louise began to move back, but he had seen her.

'Come out where I can see you. Come out!' He pulled Blair up and held the knife to her throat. 'Or I'll do her now!'

Louise stepped out. He held a torch full on her. She put up her hands to shield her eyes; she could see nothing in the sudden dazzling light.

'Come over here!'

She obeyed the command, walking slowly towards the platform where he was holding Blair. She still could not see his face, but the voice did not belong to Chris James. Their voices shared the same timbre but his had a gravelly, granular quality that Chris's lacked. It was the voice of an older man. He dropped Blair and came towards her grabbing her by the shoulder. The hand gripping her, shaking her, was roughened; it snagged the thin jersey cotton of her T-shirt; the palm was calloused by the kind of work Chris had never known. She was near enough to see his face. She was looking into the eyes of Chris's father. Large and dark, like his son's, but they lacked any kind of spark; they were cold.

He spun her round, holding his knife to her throat. He held it hard against her neck, positioned carefully over the carotid artery. Part of her brain noted that the haft was big and heavy, the blade large, broad and triangular, the tip obtuse-angled and sharp as a razor. A Stanley knife. He did not have to tell her not to struggle, even breathing hard meant taking the risk of getting sliced. He dragged her to the edge of the balcony and looked out.

'Where are the others? Where's your boss?'

'There – there aren't any others,' Louise managed to gasp out. 'I'm on my own.'

His hold on her eased for a moment and then retightened.

'Don't give me that. Where's that detective bitch? She wouldn't let you come here alone like this.'

'I didn't.' Della stepped out of the shadows. 'I'm here. Let her go.'

Quite fit for an older guy; Mandy's words came back as Della walked towards him, holding her hands out where he could see them.

'Let her go,' she repeated. 'Take me instead.'

She kept her gaze on him, but every now and then her eyes flicked to the rail behind him. Under the layers of flaking white paint, the wrought-iron tracery had corroded to the point where it was as frail as a paper doily. He had pulled Louise against it; the metal was cracking under their combined weight. Any more pressure, any sudden movement, would be enough to send them both crashing into the chasm below. Della had to get him away from it. That was why she had shown herself.

'Come on, Chris. You know it's hopeless . . .'

Della could feel him wavering. There was fear behind the heavy male sweat he was giving off, she could smell it from here. What he wanted, craved above everything else, was control, everything planned down to the last detail; and things were going badly wrong.

'Let her go. Give yourself up.'

'No!' He pulled Louise even tighter to him. Behind him the whole balcony was bulging; Della could hear it cracking. Louise stared, eyes dilating with terror. She reached behind, clutching at the ironwork, and her fingers went straight through. She could hear nothing beyond the pulse beating in her head and their own breathing, but adrenalin had heightened his awareness, allowing him to hear across space, tuning in to any noise that could not be accounted for, however distant, however small. He turned his head into the shadowed emptiness.

His grip loosened slightly as he leaned out further to gather in any sound.

'Someone's there,' he whispered. 'Who is it?'

'Dad? You heard what Della said, let her go!'

The voice, booming out of the darkness, echoed off the walls, making the origin impossible to locate. As he leaned further out, questing for his son in the swallowing darkness, his grip on the girl slackened even further. This was the chance Della had been waiting for. She leapt across the space between them, and grabbed for Louise, using all her strength to break his hold, putting herself between his knife and the girl, wrestling her out of his choking embrace. His arm came up, slashing at Della, catching her under the chin, but she had Louise now, she used her shoulder to force him backwards. The sudden violent movement was too much for the fragile ironwork. The balustrade split with a rending crack.

In seeming slow motion, Della lunged to the right, hauling Louise with her, grabbing for one of the thick barley-twist columns which extended from the floor to the roof, as a whole section of the parapet began to fall. Della put her arm round Louise, shielding her, as he pitched out into empty space, arms wide. His body jack-knifed into a piking dive and began to tumble, twisting and turning in a grotesque parody of the control he once commanded. He hit the stepped diving platforms, once, twice, before plunging past the old waterline and on to the iron stanchions and smashed panes which lay at the bottom of the empty swimming pool.

Della clung to Louise, to the pillar, embracing the flaking ironwork, tasting rust and bile mixed in her mouth, her breath coming in short shallow gasps. She stayed, hanging on like that, until she heard her name repeated in her ear, and an arm going round her. Chris James pulled her hands away from the pillar, gently releasing her fingers one by one. He took her and Louise over to Blair, taking care to keep away from the broken balcony edge, and what lay sprawled on the bottom of the pool forty feet below.

Help was not long in arriving. Police and paramedics were on the scene in minutes. They split into separate teams. One group went up to the balcony to help the living, the others climbed down into the empty swimming pool to deal with the dead. The body lay like a severed puppet, arms and legs thrown out, the neck twisted, the head at the wrong angle to the body. They knew there was nothing to be done, but it was their job to check.

Della sat on the steps outside and watched the ambulance pulling away, taking Blair and Louise to the nearest hospital. They had not been physically harmed, but they were both suffering from shock. In Blair's case this was complicated by dehydration; the girl was in a pretty bad way. The siren faded rapidly into the other late-night city sounds, but it only had a mile or so to go; they would be there soon.

'How are you?'

She looked up at Jack Ryder, staring down at her, hands in pockets.

'It's just a nick.' She dabbed at the underside of her chin. 'I'm fine for someone who has just jeopardized a young girl's life and nearly lost a client.'

'Don't be so hard on yourself. You didn't know Louise was going to wander off.'

'She shouldn't have been there in the first place.' Della held her head in her hands. 'How could I have been so stupid?'

There was no answer to that. Jack did not comment.

'I mean, how did I miss him? He was there all

the time.' Chris James senior. Standing behind Heather Griffiths in those team photos. The helpful caretaker in Kay's block of flats. The friendly porter who let Amanda McCann store her precious bicycle in his office. 'And I just looked straight through him. Couldn't see him for the son, couldn't see him for the other one. How many times has that happened? Once too many for three young women. Four, nearly. Five, if you include Louise . . .'

'Like I said, don't be too hard on yourself. We strolled right by him once or twice ourselves. I've just had a check done. He doesn't appear on any of the lists of persons interviewed.'

'How's that?' Della asked, but she knew the answer.

Heather disappeared from the *new* leisure centre. He didn't work there. Had never even been there. He left his job at the flats where Kay lived more than a year before she disappeared.

'He was only one of a number of porters who manned the lodge where Amanda left her bike,' Jack was saying. 'And, guess what? That week he was off sick.'

'You'd still have his name, though.'

'Oh, yeah.' Jack passed a hand over his face. 'Except someone wrote down "Carl" instead of "Chris". He knew about Blair through his son.' Jack shrugged. 'He was there or thereabouts each time, but it's impossible to check everyone. Do you think Chris Junior knew?'

Della shook her head. 'He says not. He led me here on a hunch, a feeling he'd got. He gave your lads the slip and I saw him leave the club so I followed him, we found the van and,' she gestured, palms wide, 'the rest you know.'

Jack rubbed the stubble lining his jaw. 'I hope he didn't, for his sake. I hope he didn't know. Hell of a thing to live with.' He paused, considering. 'Maybe with the first one, Heather, he might have had a bit of an idea, but I guess just couldn't think it was his old man. Easier to tell himself the girl had done a runner. People look away if it's someone close; it's like they can't see, don't want to notice. They'll ignore things right in their faces. They'll deny, and go on denying.'

It happened. Della knew it. She had seen it. Interviewed relatives, neighbours – child abuse cases, rapes, assaults, murders. She would read the papers and react like anyone else: how could someone shield a person like that? But in the interview room there had been times when she'd thought: *What would I do?* If I lived in a world so fragile, the truth would tear it apart. A world where the only way to survive was to lie to yourself and keep on lying, whatever the odds, whatever the cost.

'Will he be all right?'

'Rob, one of the lads, is with him now. He's a mate. He'll look after him. And then there's counselling – I'll get him help.'

'I got it wrong, Jack.' Della closed her eyes. 'I

got the wrong one. I thought it was Chris. I was so sure it was the son.'

Jack shrugged, shoving his hands deeper in his pockets. 'You got to the right place, at the right time.'

'Only just.'

'You saved her life.'

'No.' Della shook her head. 'Louise did that.'

'Yeah. I guess she did. Brave kid.'

Della had allowed herself to take a partial view. She had let her prejudices blind her to the truth. She stared down at the pavement, unable to look at him.

'Della?' He touched her shoulder.

'Yeah?'

'Blair's safe now. I don't know what he had in mind for her but my guess is, he was going to take his time. She was saved from that, and you were part of it. Now go home, get some sleep, and stop beating yourself up.' He glanced back towards the swimming pool. 'I've got to get back. They should be about ready to get the body out. Take care, Della.'

'And you.' Della stood up slowly, her body aching all over. 'Goodbye, Jack.'

'Bye, Della. I'll call you.'

He turned away from her, back to the blank façade where one of his officers was standing guard. For him, this was just the beginning. Tomorrow morning they would be taking the fabric apart, brick by brick, stone by stone, until they located the other girls, until they found the bodies. He headed up the steps, past the blue and white scene of crime tape, and into a building which, within days, would secure its place among the world's most notorious addresses.

Chapter 27

Jubilee Baths became very big news indeed. News teams came from everywhere to jostle and film outside the place where Blair Paige had been held during her kidnap. And they stayed as the horror deepened, and the bodies were found, discovered lying together, under a heap of coke, beneath a grating deep in the cellar. A police spokeswoman stood, grim faced, talking to camera while commentators translated all round her and her words were flashed around the world.

As soon as she was well enough, Blair consented to a press conference. She sat in front of the cameras, and spoke to a packed room, greedy for every detail. She appeared paler, thinner, but apart from that, none the worse for her ordeal. She was young and strong and, physically, her recovery had been swift. Louise sat with her, flanked by Gina and Felicity, but all attention was focused on Blair.

The press conference had been organized by the police, with Jack Ryder in overall charge, vetting the questions, ready to end it when he thought the girl had had enough. When the questions thinned to ones and twos, and were mostly repeating themselves, Jack stood up.

'That's all, ladies and gentlemen. I think Miss Paige has answered enough questions.'

'Wait a minute, Jack.' Blair put her hand on his arm. She had a statement in front of her, prepared for her by lawyers, advisers, PR people. She pushed it aside. 'I've got something else to say.' She leaned forward, arms on the table. 'I agreed to come here today to meet you and to answer your questions; now I want you to listen. What happened . . .' she paused, 'is not just to do with me. Three other girls died in . . . in that place. I'm no different from Heather, Kay and Amanda, and I want that fact remembered and I want them respected. I was lucky, I survived, but only because of Louise here.' Blair took her friend's hand and held it up. 'I owe her my life.'

She stood to go. Cameras flashed, and the reporters renewed their clamour as Jack Ryder escorted her out of the studio.

After this, Blair made no more public statements. Jack Ryder made sure that her visits to the bereaved families of the murdered girls were kept strictly private. Blair had wanted to meet the parents of Heather and Amanda, and had consented to speak at a memorial service for their daughters, but that would not be until the Autumn, and Blair was leaving soon, going back to LA.

Until she went, Louise would stay. They slept in the same room so her friend could be there when Blair woke from terrible dreams where she couldn't breathe, where she lay helpless, taped, bound and hooded in suffocating darkness. She could not see the face of her attacker, only hear his voice, crooning what he would do to her, over and over. Louise listened to her sobbing out her terror, reliving it night after night. She held her and understood. She had dreams of her own. Being there for each other was part of the healing process.

Blair's physical ordeal had ended on that hot July night but it would take time to cure the rest of her. The memories were lodged like splinters in the mind; they would have to be removed one at a time. She was going to need help with that, and Gina was ready to pay any amount for the best treatment, the best therapy. She knew what her daughter needed, if she was ever going to appear on the screen again, but to get that they had to go back to California.

Blair pleaded with Louise to go with her; so did Gina. Blair's mother had suffered cruelly, almost as much as Blair herself, and the experience had changed her. She was quieter, more subdued. Certainly her attitude towards Louise had changed completely. She now regarded the girl as another daughter, had practically offered to adopt her.

'You saved her life,' was all she'd said when they met in the hospital, her voice shaking with gratitude. 'I owe everything to you.'

It did not take Louise long to decide that her place could not be permanently at Blair's side. She had her own life, her own family, and no matter how strong their friendship, Louise did not belong in Blair's world; she would always be overshadowed by the other girl. Her ambitions lay in different directions; she had to go back to school.

'You must come in your holidays then, bring your family. You now have a second home with us in LA,' Gina said to her, and meant it.

It was an offer Louise would take up in the future but, for now, her place would be taken by Stephen. His relationship with Penny was over and he planned to transfer to a medical school in California. After all that had happened, he wanted to be with Blair. Despite their problems in the past, she needed him by her now. He was someone she could trust and his being there would help with Gina. Louise thought, privately, that it was her mother, not Blair, who most needed therapy.

'I'll look after both of them. Don't you worry,' he said, and Louise believed him. Blair had told her that she felt safer with him than anyone else. Except for Della.

'I don't know why.' The detective gave a mirthless laugh. 'Putting your trust in me nearly cost you your life.'

'You were there when I needed you.'

'More by luck than judgement.'

'That doesn't matter. You were there.'

Della had been called because there was something Blair wanted to do before she went, someone she wanted to see before she left for America. She wanted to see Chris again.

The news reports had spoken of 'unfathomable

evil' behind the terrible crimes, there had been extensive speculation about Mr James Snr., but the only person who could possibly guess why, guess what might have gone on in his father's mind, was Chris, and so far his son had not said a word. He had been offered large sums of money for his version of events but he wasn't talking to anybody.

He had given up his job at The Greswoldes and seemed to have dropped out of circulation completely, but Della found him without much difficulty, working on an inner-city youth project. At first he wouldn't even speak to her, but in those crucial moments in the stinking hell of that darkened pool, the two of them had come to some kind of unspoken understanding, had struck up some kind of rapport.

'What does she want to see me for?' he asked her.

Della shrugged. 'Just wants to talk to you.'

'What about?'

'I don't know. That's between you and her.'

'I can't, Della. I'm too ashamed, that's the truth of it. My own father . . . I honest to God didn't know. Not till the last minute when I was in the club looking down at the street and thinking about Heather; it wasn't until then that it really clicked into place.' He shook his head. 'When I think about how I led Blair to him, it was down to me, through me.' He placed a hand on his chest. 'I made it possible for him to get that close in. It makes me sick.'

Della nodded, arms folded. She could understand his feelings.

'I know it's tough, Chris,' she said, eventually. 'But if you love her, you have to tell her all this. You owe it to her. Tell her what you've told me, tell her everything, what he was like when you were a kid, everything. She needs to know as much as possible if she is to really come to terms with her experience. You can help her, help her make sense of it.'

Chris agreed to accompany Della back to London. The detective took him to the flat and left the two of them alone. They were together for over two hours and then Chris left. Blair never mentioned what was spoken between them, she kept it private, but she thought a lot about what he'd said to her. 'Don't fight it, use it,' were his parting words, 'in your acting, in the roles you play. Like a boxer, like a sportsman, channel the anger, the aggression, the fear and humiliation. You can get it out of yourself that way.' It was good advice. It helped. Gradually the nightmares began to fade.

The day of Blair's departure for the States saw a marked change in the weather. It was an early flight and the morning was cold, tinged with autumn, as Della accompanied Louise to the airport to see them off. Blair and Louise hugged and promised to keep in touch; phoning and writing would keep them together until they could see each other next summer. Blair hugged Della, too, thanking her again. Even Gina stepped forward to shake the detective by the hand and say:

'Thank you for my daughter. I must apologize. I was wrong about you.'

She went through the barriers then, leaving Felicity to manage the hand luggage. The PA's eyes widened and she smiled as she, too, said goodbye to Della. There had to be a first for everything. She could not recall having heard Gina admit she was wrong, or apologize, ever in her life before.

Blair took her seat in first class. She always sat by the window; she liked to look at whatever was out there, even if it was just clouds and ocean. She fastened her seatbelt and settled herself down, putting on her Walkman against the growing whine of the 747 engines.

As the big plane began to turn and taxi for take-off, she glanced out of the window to look at England for one last time. They were moving now, passing along the length of the terminal building. The sky was grey, heavily overcast; a cold gusting wind and the threat of rain had kept most people off the roof-top viewing platform. Most people. There was one person, standing right at the end, leaning on the barrier, wind tugging his shirt, blowing his black hair away from his face. As the plane began to move towards its take-off proper, Blair turned her head, twisting round to keep him in view. It was Chris James, his hand held in farewell.

Blair knew it was stupid, he could not possibly see her, but as the plane accelerated to take-off speed, as it left the runway, leaving the land behind, she found herself looking down, searching for his dwindling figure, her own hand up against the reinforced plastic surface of the window, trying in vain to return his salute.

Also by Celia Rees

Colour Her Head

1968. The savage murder of six-year-old Jennifer Beresford turns the Summer of Love into a nightmare of suspicion and hate for the village of Coombe Ashleigh. A wall of silence grows up round the crime. Myth and rumour feed its notoriety.

In a junk shop, over twenty-five years later, Jude Hughes finds beads worn by the child the day she died. Jude and her friend Emma begin their own investigation, but *The Beresford Case* has remained unsolved for more than two decades and someone's prepared to kill to keep it that way . . .

The Bailey Game

Every school has places that you can find if you want to, if you don't want people to see you, if you need somewhere private. That had been important in the Bailey Game – privacy and being secret.

The Bailey Game was vicious, it wrecked people's lives. But two years ago, it was all anyone in Alex's class thought or talked about. Until one terrifying day in early spring. What happened then should have been enough to stop anyone wanting to play the Game again – ever.

Now a new girl, Lauren Price, has arrived at the school. She is new, she is different, and she comes from somewhere else. That is enough. The Bailey Game is about to start.

Alex finds she has some tough choices to make in a world where being on the outside can be dangerous . . .

Chris Crutcher
The Secrets of Sarah Byrnes

Sarah Byrnes is one hell of a friend.

They've been outcasts together since junior school – fat Moby and scarface Sarah Byrnes. They've grown up hard-nosed, streetwise and tough. They had to. So why has Sarah suddenly gone off the rails?

Desperate to help his sick friend, Moby sets out to discover what really lies behind the scars, and finds himself plunged into a shadowy world of violence, fear and abuse.

Suddenly Sarah isn't the only one in danger . . .